Milk the Fruit

edited by Bryan Caron

Phoenix Moirai LLC | Gilbert | Arizona

Phoenix Moirai LLC
1525 S. Higley Rd., Suite 104
Gilbert, AZ 85296
phoenixmoirai.com

Milk the Fruit: Whimsillusion Project Anthology #1

Introduction

A character named Bruce.
The name Sarafina.
An egg.
A cabin.
A reptile.
A fight.
The line: "Milk the fruit with care."

What do these seven things have in common? Nothing at all except each of the authors in this anthology had to use them in their stories in some form or another. That is the concept behind the Whimsillusion Project.

This little experiment went through many iterations before finally landing on the final idea. It all started with a desire to challenge writers (myself included) into something different; something outside of our comfort zones. Something to push creativity to its limits.

Once we had the bone structure set in place—an anthology of short stories (or novellas; after all, we never nitpick about word counts) written in whatever genre the author desired, but which must include seven specific items in whatever form the author chooses—it came down to, what items will the author need to include?

This couldn't be just any type of item. As I said, we

wanted to challenge everyone who submitted; give them something that would stimulate and spark the imagination (and, if I can be so bold, trigger a path forward in another WIP they've been struggling with). Bottom line, we had to come up with something fun, out-of-the-box, yet capable of offering the freedom to place in any genre, format, and style.

Authors were allowed to make these items as important or inconsequential as needed. What type of fight would it be? What kind of reptile would slither across the page? Is Sarafina a person or something else entirely? And what genre would they choose?

That last question couldn't have been answered better, as we ended up with five different genres: science fiction, fantasy, murder mystery, supernatural comedy, and political thriller.

And this is just the start! Our goal is to turn this wild experiment into a yearly anthology. Which begs even more questions: Where will volume two take us? What items will be included in future editions? And who will be brave enough to take up the challenge? Only time will tell. Until then, enjoy the works of art this first crop of brilliant authors were able to produce with seven simple items.

—*Bryan Caron*
October 2025

Table of Contents

The Herpetologist

Megan Nicole Mann

With a Bachelor of Science in Zoology, a profession looking after the wilder things of the world, and an eye for the fantasy in reality, Megan Nicole Mann debuts on the literary scene with The Herpetologist.

A life spent exploring vistas from the Great Lakes, to the Appalachian Mountains, to the Great Plains and the Atlantic coast has fueled her love for the natural world first-hand, something that informs just about everything she writes.

When not hard at work on her next story or tending to the wild things in her care, she is often seen crafting, playing a musical instrument, or exploring some new subject that has captured her curiosity.

It was a day much like most. Not a particularly riveting start to a story, but it was the truth of the matter. Dr. Beck was leaning back at his desk, expecting the regular crowd of zero students to come calling during his office hours. Feet propped upon the old, wooden thing, mug of cheap tea in hand, and glasses hardly hanging onto his nose as he read listlessly over another round of peer comments on his latest findings, he was feeling distinctly miffed. It was due, in no small part, to the fact that this would make a baker's dozen of times he'd been sent back this particular paper. Always, always, always, something had to be wrong, implausible, unsupported. What were these reviewers to know? Was pioneering research not meant to be shaped with a stone knife: rustic and explorable? He was unappreciated in his time.

Just as he felt he might actually doze off, the most peculiar of things stole his attention: a loud knock. Lolling his head toward the shabby, warped door, he had the mind to ignore it. But the knocking came again and, this time, with a voice.

"Dr. Beck? Are you there, sir?" came the muffled question of a young woman as determined as she was unsure of herself. Second row, five seats from the center, attending Theoretical Evolution and Sauropsids, she answered her fair bit of questions—asked far less, but they never failed to entertain his thoughts.

"And suppose I am?" he called back, his voice dull as the beige walls. Good lord, he needed to escape those walls.

"Oh, it's... well I've a question."

"Bold of you to assume I have an answer."

"Well, that's just it, sir. I'm curious if you even do." The confidence grew in her voice and managed to put some life back into his spine. He cocked his head at her. "May I come in? It'll make more sense if I can." Curiouser and curiouser...

"Yes, by all means. Let's see if you can stump me," he said without an ounce of derision. He slid his feet from his desk and sat up, slapping his bullied work down onto the scuffed and scratched desk top to allow his fingers to knit with anticipation.

In walked the young woman—Druce; he believed her name to be, Phoenicia Druce—dressed in her subtly eccentric way, looking to be carrying some sort of box wrapped beneath the flowing fabric of her cardigan. She appeared nervous in her movements, but not with the nerves of a student worried with making themself a fool in front of their professor. Rather, he thought he saw her steal a glance over her shoulder before shutting the door as swiftly and softly as any could, seemingly... concerned about something. Theirs was hardly a university known for unsavory activity—well, beyond the typical larceny that taught the freshmen not to leave their bags unattended—so such skittish behavior was certainly striking.

As she sped up to his desk, she looked this way and that, like a ferret at its den. "So sorry to bother you, Dr. Beck," she said as she approached, "but I wasn't sure... well, I figured you were the one to talk to about this."

"This being...?" he prompted her with a rolling gesture of his wrist.

"Well..." She set the box down on the desk, right atop his discarded paper. "It all started with my cat going missing."

He raised his eyebrows, stuffing a scoff behind a clearing of his throat. "Your... cat, Ms. Druce?"

"Yes, pay attention." That was nearly a snap; he was just as nearly impressed. "He disappeared a week ago. Three or four days isn't that weird, but—not the point. Anyway, he'd been gone too long, so I went looking around his usual haunts and, well, I found something that makes me think I won't be finding him again."

"Something beyond the realm of normal possibility?" he questioned dryly, slightly startled by the grave, some-what haunted nod he received in response. Her eyes locked onto his with intensity. Fear more potent than grief was certainly a sight. "I see... Perhaps I should take this with some serious consideration." Pushing his glasses up, he reached for the lid of the box. Unbarred from doing so, he opened the thing and saw the source of her fears.

Simply put, it was skin—or at least, it appeared to be. An opaque sheet of skin, seemingly of a scaled texture, laid across the bottom of the box. On initial inspection, it looked to be nothing but the kind of sample that would earn a prize grade for the student who'd bring it into him: impressively large and clearly textured. Only, the grain of the scales seemed to be odd—larger than typical and more similar in shape and array to that of a snake, but the feel was far less like the crisp, papery feel of a snake's shed and more like the soft, slightly rubbery coat that would strip from a gecko.

As he picked it up to get a closer look, he discovered the little fact that finally forced him to share her terror. It unfolded. The sheet of skin wasn't a regular shape but nearly twice the size of the shoebox. A torn piece of reptilian skin fit to draw a roadmap on: yes, he'd say Ms. Druce had cause for concern. Of course, being who he was, Dr. Beck's own flabbergasted horror turned to chattering exhilaration, complete with a manic smile.

"My dear girl! Do you have any idea what we have here? My condolences to your cat, but a creature this size would've hardly found him to be a meal. I say! You simply must tell me where you found this!"

"Do... do you know what it's from?" she asked, wringing her hands.

"Absolutely no clue." He leaned in. "Isn't that thrilling? I'll have to get to the bottom of this at once!" Folding the delicate treasure of a specimen back into the box, he spun wild theories around his head. At last! Something worth writing about! And it wouldn't require him to so much as reference a colleague's paper! Sweet, sweet music.

Jumping to his feet, Dr. Beck felt lighter than air, wanting to run right out that door without so much as a notepad or camera. Of course, one glance at the grim statue standing across from his desk reminded him he should probably keep his elation in check. After all, the girl had come to him regarding what she believed to be a monster that had killed her cat—hardly something anyone should be excited about. Then again, she came to him, so she had to have known. He wasn't particularly one to put many pennies into the pity department. Still, if she got too offended, she might leave without telling him what he needed to know.

With a clear of his throat, he threw a hasty tarp of composure upon himself and readdressed the distressed Ms. Druce. "Forgive me: the scientist's muse and all that. Where did you say this skin was found?"

Phoenicia Druce blinked at him like one waking from a most disappointing dream as she gave her answer. "The marsh. Out by the old lighthouse islands. There's an old cabin there—"

"Yes, I know the one," he cut her off without a thought beyond *that can't be right*. He'd had that region surveyed countless times, knew the fauna well enough to recite the total findings in his sleep. Even the typical invasives were understood ad nauseum, complete with all the particular ways each of them royally ruined the ecosystem. Of course, he couldn't recall the last time he'd actually accompanied his class out there to do it—the tedium and all—but the results had been as consistent and expectedly varied as ever for time rememberable. "Good lord…" the lawsuits he could've narrowly missed. "Ms. Druce, I am ever so glad you brought this to my attention. I'll be canvassing the area personally and, if you'd be so kind, I'll be needing an assistant—"

"Nope."

"Excuse me?"

"Forgive me, sir, but there's a reason I didn't apply for your particular internship," said Ms. Druce with a frankness that cut to the bone deeper than any sharp tongue or scolding rebuke could have. "I do thank you for looking into this and will be sure to alert the authorities to your last known whereabouts, should you go missing." With a nod and a none too amiable smile, she turned and left his office, shutting the door with the same careful quiet as she'd come.

Utterly affronted, Dr. Beck snorted and looked to the box of skin, as if it could offer him any consolation. In truth, he didn't need an assistant—not for preliminary scouting anyway—but it could only have been to her benefit to have her name stuck to this endeavor. How ungrateful. Oh well. She could go cry about her cat to whichever professor she preferred. It was no loss to him.

Preparations were quick, simple, light. If it weren't for the mounting spring heat, he wouldn't have even thought to bring a water bottle. All he needed was his single, small trail sack with his camera and note things—oh, and a fair amount of fluid for cleaning his glasses. Those godforsaken gnats could cause quite the blindness to the visually challenged.

Dressed well in his waders and bucket hat, Dr. Beck drove out to the deserted, gravel lot that marked the entrance to the "nature trail," as it were. Of course, without waders, it was hardly a trail to walk. It had been no small pleasure of his to watch his students ignore his warnings about such once upon a time. To one as seasoned as himself, it might as well have been a paved trail through fairyland.

Dr. Beck hardly noticed the pull of the mud as it tried to suck him down into the mire, nor the buzz of the various invertebrates that swarmed him. It wasn't his place to complain about such things. Besides, he was in their country and it was only to one's benefit to move and tolerate the countrymen.

The air was full of frog song, insect chatter, and the distant rhythm of crashing waves. An occasional crane would come crying past, landing to spear whatever unfortunate morsel it had happened to spot in the murky water. All lovely, all ordinary, and all decidedly not indicative of there being some disturbance of the gigantic sort lumbering around beneath the arrow-shaped leaves. The aforementioned cabin had yet to appear, so it was entirely possible that he wasn't yet close enough, but a creature that large would surely have a large hunting ground.

Onward he slogged until patches of solid ground grew in frequency and the waters grew ever deeper. Marsh would become lakeshores before too long, but sooner still did it seem he'd be walking into a dead zone.

The soggy symphony faded behind him, becoming increasingly distant as he plowed forward. As he eased down into a deep, dark stream he knew to be home of some of the larger turtles he had no desire to meet on their terms, he became horrifically conscious of the silence. Not a bird flew here, no wayward squirrel dared to bark at him, there was not hair or hide of a single creature beyond whatever microorganisms drifted through the muck. Climbing up the opposite bank, he stopped to take a look around, a hot, humid breeze rolling over his shoulders. Beyond the silence, he noticed nothing amiss. No tracks, no scars on any tree bark, no turned earth—it was all perfectly pristine. That was, of course, with the exception of the cabin he saw in the distance.

He'd been there before. It was a dilapidated thing, suited more to termites and indulgent deer than human habitation as it leaned heavily against the aged trees at its side. The closer he got to the mossy, rotten thing, the more he looked, and the same he saw. There was nothing out of the ordinary beyond the vacancy of wildlife. By the time he reached the doorless doorstep of the cabin—its moist, mildewy odor offensive to the near point of being intoxicating—he felt he should give up this inane adventure. After all, Ms. Druce had been far too eager to leave him to his own devices and, if he did say so himself, a little too calm about losing her beloved cat, even with the added sting of his callous impropriety on the subject. It was looking increasingly likely that she, and probably a few of her fellow miffed students, had decided to put him up to a snipe chase. So much for the excitement of discovery.

With a deflating, irritated sigh, he plopped down onto the nearest stream bank, where he toyed listlessly with the surface of the subtly flowing water. It and the whispering wind were the only things to be heard, at least until the tiniest of splashes stole his attention. The brilliant, green flash of a leopard frog jumped from the murky water right onto his hand. Ever so gently, he lifted the amphibious beauty to better appreciate it. Funny, he'd seen so many of these little ones, he'd assumed he'd grown tired of them, but it was ever too evident that he never would. When it hopped away, back into the inky, umber shallows, he felt his heart drop.

As a boy, he would've cradled the spotted specimen and ferried it home—a use for his moss and stones at last. And how he would've curated that river-wrought furniture. The simplest of salamanders had lived like kings under his watch, the most common of toads, and pest-thought anoles... Well, he'd done his best. It was a delicate thing, caring for creatures that could breathe and drink through their skin, and so it had been quite the learning curve. Lizards were a far better place to start, though deceptively delicate in their own right. Learning curve... he'd long forgotten how many trials and errors it had taken, but it had never been work, not really (though it had certainly taken effort).

With a mind to head home and check on his current terrariums, Dr. Beck rose from the muddy bank, then promptly froze. Something stirred behind him; something larger. It had come from the cabin. The thought of his terrariums and the rather large, wooden hides he had for his biggest specimens came to mind.

Slowly, praying the mud beneath him would hold, he turned on his spine to glance toward the sound. Steeling his nerve, he allowed his feet to follow his gaze and headed toward the shadowy, rotting thing. As he neared, the noise came again: a soft rustling, something's feet or sides against a wet nest of leaves. It gave him pause, but only for a moment. This was what he'd come here for.

He stepped inside.

A shadow darted at him, hissing and spitting.

Sheer panic shot through him as he flailed backward like a startled pigeon, his mind flipping rapidly through the various creatures whose fangs could cause him harm in those woods. His rash movements cost him his footing. Down he went, landing hard with a resounding *splat* into the mud and moss, his tailbone managing to find the one stone among the sodden soil. If this was more than a bluff, he was done for.

The creature hopped onto his lap, claws-first, growling, posturing... *hackling.*

It was a cat. A most striking cat—and mammals seldom deserved the honor of such a compliment—its coat a delicately dappled brown, save for its impossibly voluminous tail, which looked to have been stitched on from another cat of a frostier coloration. It stared him down with its impossibly blue eyes, their pupils gigantic voids that nearly robbed them of the rich color. Looking at it, he couldn't help but laugh. The poor thing was terrified and, undoubtedly, missing a certain Ms. Druce.

"So, there's the beast of the hour," said Dr. Beck to the feline past his relieved laughter. "Well, I suppose that settles it then, doesn't it? There's no colossal cat-eater out here, is there? What a shame."

The thing relaxed its claws—harmless against his waders besides—and loosened its posture. But it was still far from pleased, its snowy tail twitching this way and that.

"Oh, do lighten up. A cat is far too inefficient a meal for me to condone any reptile to feed on such a thing. I mean, look at you." He reached for the cat, but it hopped away, hissing again. "You're nothing but fur."

Standing up, he made up his mind to reach again for the perilous pet—cats were a scourge on the marsh after all—but the fickle feline slipped from his reach twice over again. He pursued, refusing to be outdone by an oversold furball, following it straight into the dark of the cabin.

"Honestly," he grumbled as it hopped up onto the remains of a dilapidated chair. "This is getting quite red—oh…"

His eyes were stolen (and his mind captivated) by the sight he beheld over to the right of the festering furniture, nestled beside the sagging dining table. They were a sight so familiar and yet impossibly foreign: the dirty, ivory-colored, oblong objects he'd examined countless times from countless species. That is to say, they were eggs and, upon closer inspection—as he was irresistibly drawn without care or consideration for his own wellbeing—of the expected leathery, flexible texture of those belonging to something reptilian in nature. More specifically, they looked to belong to a lizard or a snake. The only issue he took was the fact that they were massive. Each was larger than the cat by a fair margin. By estimation, he figured they may weigh beyond twenty pounds apiece, though he wouldn't dare pick one up. Even he wasn't so eager as to abandon sense to that degree.

All he could do was stare in dumbstruck disbelief as he straightened up to back away. This was beyond anything anyone had cataloged, even in a paleontological context. At best, this could've been some sort of kiwi bird situation—

which would make this a most unfortunate creature—but his instincts told him otherwise. Instinct was the guiding light of successful inquiry as much as the bane that hindered discovery, so it was always a difficulty to decide whether to listen to it, but Dr. Beck wasn't so sure it mattered in this instance. Even a creature so unfortunate as the kiwi bird would be beyond the size of the largest of crocodiles to carry such an egg… especially so many. He hoped to the heavens this wasn't a communal nest.

"I… do believe we should be making ourselves scarce, my furry friend," said Dr. Beck to the cat, not taking his eyes off of the eggs. "Discoveries of this nature are best made armed."

Dr. Beck made no more than a step back before a dreaded sound stopped him and startled the cat to darting toward his feet, hissing toward whatever evil was behind him while using him as a shield. Such was a sort of sound that needed no investigation and it belonged to no house cat. That was the bellowing hiss of a large lizard—a very large lizard. The signature scent of putrid meat carried on the wind of its breath. Hissing himself through a grimace, he braced for the one hail Mary of a hair-brained tactic he could use to maybe survive this.

Quick as a whip, he spun around, roaring a shout with all he had despite his dry throat and flipping stomach as he threw his arms far above his head. The roar devolved quickly into a genuine scream of fear as his wide eyes fell on the gigantic monitor. It was eye to eye with him, relaxed—no, borderline bored as it looked back at him with half-closed eyes and a level hunch to its neck. Either this was going better for him than he ever could've hoped or it was going so poorly that he might as well have been a beetle before a boot.

Without a change to its posture, the creature bellowed again and Dr. Beck's legs buckled, collapsing him onto the cabin floor. The cat jumped into his lap—whether in a desperate bid for comfort or as some idiotically valiant attempt at bravery, he couldn't have said—and both were left staring up at what was likely to be their demise.

The monitor gave a flick of its forked, purple tongue and stared down at them with hardly a tilt of its head. It seemed there was a disdain in its silvery eye—a nearly human disdain—as if their roles had been reversed and it was Dr. Beck looking down at some screaming lizard that had gotten in the way of his work for lack of under-standing that he wasn't there to cause harm. Of course, he wasn't about to put money down on the idea that this thing meant him no harm. He wasn't about to put money down on anything anymore. Such a hulking herptile belonged in his greatest dreams or worst nightmares, not looking down at him like gum on a desk. Clearly, scien-tific postulation had missed a few considerations.

With a slow blink, the creature lowered its head, causing Dr. Beck to scramble back out of pure instinctive fear. The monitor paused, releasing a gravely hiss that sounded strikingly like an exasperated sigh. It darted one of its massive feet toward him, hooking his waders with its talons and dragging him forward. Dr. Beck screamed as he was dragged, the cat leaping to try and burrow down his shirt. Both were plucked off the mossy floor by the back of the waders and carried off like a misbehaving kitten scruffed by its mother.

All the professor could do was clutch the trembling cat to his chest from where it hid between his outer and undershirt, hardly feeling the sting of its claws poking at his skin as he swayed over the marsh floor. His own panic was only kept in check by focusing on what he could analyze, such as how on earth such a large varandian could move with the silent ease of a large cat. Its splayed toes hardly made a squelch on the wettest of soil. How long he was hulled away like that, he couldn't have said, but they were approaching the lakeshore quickly and the sudden fear that drowning might be a more likely fate than being torn to shreds was beginning to creep in. As stones and chunks of sun-bleached, wood became smaller and smaller, pebbles turned to a dark approximation of sand soaked with the smell of mussels, he could feel his fate drawing nearer.

When the time came for those massive talons and toes to vanish beneath the murky, gray water, the monitor stopped, bringing Dr. Beck's swinging to a lurching stop. Here it was, the moment of truth; would he be drowned, shredded, or some sadistic combination of the two? What he had failed to consider was the apparent third option—he was thrown. The great lizard rotated its head back, then snapped it forward like a sling, launching Dr. Beck out across the lake, screaming as he spun like a human discus.

The air was stunned from his lungs as his body slapped down onto the water, face and belly first. Unable to breathe, the cat probably dead, he floated there like a hapless piece of driftwood until a distinctly irritable nudge flipped him over. He felt something grab onto his leg like a vice. His breath slowly returned to him as he was dragged along by the monitor, daring to cast the colossal creature a look. Honestly, if he hadn't been in peril, he would've been stunned with the pure awe he found in its movements, the water glistening off its marbled skin as it stretched and shifted over those powerful muscles. Of course, he was in peril, and he couldn't help but wonder where this thing was taking him.

His attention was stolen from his captor when a sharp pain stabbed his chest. Looking down toward it, he saw the sodden form of the dappled cat poke its head out from under his shirt, wheezing and panting as it looked at him like it was seeing stars. Well, at least he wouldn't die alone.

Once again, the time grew immeasurable but did eventually come to a head. There was no pause this time; no wind up before the launching. No, the intentions of the lizard were long telegraphed as it grew faster and faster to the point that the professor's head started skipping like a stone off the surface of the water, until the water fell away altogether.

For a moment, they soared through the air until they suddenly weren't and Dr. Beck was seeing stars. His head kept going as the monitor slammed to a stop, causing the latter to meet the broadside of something hard and likely wooded. The stars cleared from his eyes just in time for his glasses to try and abandon him, some deep-seated reflex allowing him to catch the traitorous things just in time. Absolutely not. If they'd managed to make it that far with him—which he couldn't say for his hat or bag—they did not get to jump ship now. Speaking of ships, who would've guessed where this creature dragged him?

Up, over, and onto the hard, hollow floor, the professor was dragged and dropped, landing on what turned out to be some sort of ship. Of course it was—what other large, wooden thing would a gigantic monitor lizard have dragged him out through the middle of a lake to? In all seriousness, though he couldn't help the increasingly cynical humor buzzing through his head, a look around at the structure of the thing—masts, decks, and all—gave away what he was picking himself up off of the floor of.

The cat dared to pop up even further, placing its paws on the stretched-out collar of his soaked shirt and making him feel much like a bizarre kangaroo. Might as well, though the smell of wet fur being shoved into his nose was a step too far, so he pulled the drowned rat from his shirt and stuck it with a surprising amount of ease into his waders instead. If he must be a kangaroo, the least he owed himself was his choice of pouch.

The cat situated and nerves officially shot to the point of numbness, the professor looked here and there across the ship, which was in no poor shape, shocked to find no crew. At least, he couldn't have. The absurdity if he had would've been a tick too far, he thought, for he saw no sailors, but he saw plenty a living thing.

All over the decks, up the masts, pulling at the tack lines—not working, no, perish the thought of it—there were gigantic monitors of the like standing beside him. Some of them, though, looked a fair bit more impressive, sporting horns, spines, frills, and sails that were most ridiculously uncharacteristic of the family. All had unique patterns to their scales in a variety of colors, though none were too brilliant.

Increasingly, this was feeling like some sort of fevered dream that had escaped his childhood. Perhaps some particularly spiteful student had slipped something into his tea when he hadn't been looking. Although, the full body aches from being tossed and dragged were hard to write off to the realm of hallucination. That was, of course, unless he wasn't asleep and merely actually hallucinating.

So dazed was he by all this that he had nearly forgotten the now considerably less impressive monitor standing beside him. So senseless, in fact, that, when he turned to look back at his sour-faced captor, he forgot himself instead.

"The pretty boys send you to do their dirty work then, do they?" Dr. Beck snorted at the massive monitor

With heavy eyelids, the great lizard seemed to glare at him, huffing a hiss as it whipped a short flick of its tongue. The professor nearly lost his feet as it swung the tip of its tail to whack him across his lower back, maintaining pressure as it jerked its head in a general direction and started walking. Dr. Beck tossed a shrugging look down to the cat, giving it a pat on its head as he obliged the beast. It wasn't as if there was much of a choice but to comply, besides.

It quickly became apparent that the drab monitor was leading him to the cabin at the stern of the vessel, its claws click-clacking and scraping along with a notable trudging weight. He thought he may have caught a glare from one of the frilled monitors off to the side as it paused, middeck waxing, but couldn't have said for sure. Besides, they soon reached the doors and all else was far less important.

The monitor paused and, with a deep breath and a shake of his head—Dr. Beck could've sworn a roll of the eye as well—it raised one of its massive, spindly-toed feet, seemingly to wrap on the doors. They flung wide before it had the chance, leaving Dr. Beck jumping back like a startled cat as he clutched the actual one tight against his chest. The monitor, unsurprisingly, appeared unsurprised, slowly lowering its foot back to the floor.

"No, no, no! You have to—no! How many times do I have to say it? Milk the fruit with care, or else you'll wind up crushing the seeds into the milk. The last thing we need is the resulting aphrodisiac—wait what?"

You would think every event up to this point would have prepared Dr. Beck for what he was witnessing, but you would be, remarkably, wrong.

Before him stood a woman with her back to him and head turned as far over her shoulder as she could manage, a much thinner lizard—remarkably wearing glasses, because of course it was—visible over her other shoulder inside the cabin with a glowing bunch of bulbous fruit around its neck and a single claw pointed toward him. Optically-challenged, fruit-bearing lizard aside, the woman stole the show here. She was dressed in the most unequivocally absurd and garish bit of gaudy clothing he had ever seen—and he used the term "clothing" lightly here, so much so that her ensemble earned a wrinkle of the nose, and it only got worse as she turned around. Feathers, that was it. Feathers, feathers, and more feathers in a nauseating array of colors bright enough to burn the retinas, and of lengths, shapes, and sizes the professor was certain couldn't be real. He could hardly define a skirt, bodice, or the like, for it was all just feathers, complete with a draping cloak that looked to mimic wings. Honestly, he was to the point where he might've believed they were growing from her very skin if many wouldn't have been pointing in the wrong direction.

"Ack! Bruno! How *dare* you interrupt us! You know how she..." the plumed woman trailed off as the drab monitor gestured a foot, most unenthusiastically, toward Dr. Beck. "Oh! Well, you should've spoken up sooner. And who might this be?" She leaned in with a much too... interested look upon her face.

Taking a step back, the professor introduced himself. "Hmm. Well, ma'am, I'm Doctor Bruce Beck of Mentor University, and I—"

"Doctor, did you say?" she chirped, looking up at him with almost frighteningly wide eyes and an impossibly toothy smile. "A medical man?"

"Uh, no, a doctor of herpetology and theoretical taxonomy..." he corrected with all the indignance such an assumption deserved. As if a doctor of medicine would dare wet their toes in the marsh.

"Hmm. Can't say I understand a lick of what you just said but, either way, Brucey, I wasn't talking to you," she said with such a blithe air as to make his skin prickle like he'd been tossed into a burning cactus, "I was talking to this little morsel." She poked the cat on the nose, earning a well-deserved growl.

"As if he wants to tell you," scoffed the professor as he turned to remove the cat from her reach. It wasn't as if he knew the answer to her question, but this impertinent lunatic didn't deserve the satisfaction of knowing that bit. "And, for your information, I only told you my full name as a professional courtesy. Not even my friends are permitted to call—"

"Whatever, Brucey. Who either of you are hardly matters…" The madwoman cut him off like she was lazily swatting a fly from her ear. "Come to think of it, Bruno, why on earth did you drag them here? You know the quota's been filled." She planted her hands on her hips as she questioned the drab monitor, who was looking increasingly finished with this interaction by the second.

Shutting its eyes, it licked its chops, then tuned slowly to look at Dr. Beck, wearing a distinctly expectant expression. Did it really think he'd out himself for whatever crime he'd apparently committed? Well, he knew what the crime was—it didn't take a genius to figure that most giant reptiles probably weren't a fan of strangers poking around their eggs—but why would he ever say? Evidently, the monitor caught onto the fact. It was altogether likely that it had known its plea had been a long shot from the jump, drooping its head before swinging it back toward the feathered menace. The lizard—Bruno, it seemed his name was—began to mime out some vague gestures that Dr. Beck couldn't begin to translate, even as one who knew what was trying to be said. At any rate, it seemed that Feathers over there didn't have that problem, nodding with a brow furrowed in contemplation as Bruno finished his account.

"I see…" She snapped her gaze, shored up to narrow daggers, toward Dr. Beck. "What brought you to the cabin, Brucey?" She stepped forward with a pronounced thud. "What were you hoping to do, Brucey?"

The sheer waves of intimidation this woman managed to give off should've been impossible. It was so ridiculous that Dr. Beck caught himself blurting a laugh before managing to reign it in. There was something incredibly off about her, beyond the obvious fact that several screws were loose or missing, and he had the distinct gut feeling that he shouldn't find out just what it was. So, naturally, he had to worm his way out.

"Well, Ms—I'm sorry, but I don't believe I've had the pleasure of knowing your name." The cordiality tasted like cheap medicine on his tongue; he hadn't spoken that way since his assistantship days.

"Eve." She answered sharply with none of the same courtesy. How beastly.

"Well, Ms. Eve," he continued, managing a smile despite the desire to sneer, "I am merely a humble scientist interested in the scaled and slippery things of this world— of course meaning those like your friend here." He gestured to Bruno, who he swore managed another eye roll. "As such, naturally—"

"Oh…! *That's* what you meant!" Eve bowled right over his words again, this time with a snap of her fingers and a rekindled sense of intrigue to replace the suspicion. "You academic types really oughtta learn to get to the point. If you'd just said so—"

"Speaking of getting to the point," Dr. Beck returned her manners, mockingly matching her blithe smile, "I'd love to get to the point of why I'm here. Or, quite frankly, to knowing where here even is."

The bizarre woman didn't seem offended so much as confused, standing there, blinking at him like her thoughts had stalled out behind her eyes. She turned to Bruno, who looked thoroughly checked out of the conversation, then back to him, hand on her chin, finger tapping her nose.

"Y'know, Brucey—"

"I told you not to—"

"*Y'know*, Brucey," she carried on. "Bruno has a particular job and I'm not sure you'd like to know what it is."

"Clearly, he's a guardian," said Dr. Beck flatly, absentmindedly playing with the cat's damp fur, nearly having forgotten the sodden furball pouched in his waders.

"Quite wrong," she giggled, sounding much too pleased with herself. "Which I'm gathering you haven't been told quite enough in your life."

"And I'm gathering you haven't been told 'no' nearly enough either, but I wasn't about to get personal," he derided cooly, casting the cat a glance to see if it shared in his irritation. It looked decidedly irritable, but that could hardly be blamed on impolite conversation.

"Heh… indeed," she said, looking him up and down. "But enough of that. Brucey, was it?"

"You've… you've used my—how many times—?"

"Allow me to welcome you aboard the Sarafina!"

Feeling like his brains might start leaking from his ears at any second, Dr. Beck started glancing and gesturing around for anyone that might spare him some patience, for his were utterly spent. With a deep breath that he might as well have been sucking through a straw, he straightened his grimy glasses and resolved not to be broken down by this impish, feathered woman.

"And to what do I owe the honor?" he asked through the gritted teeth of his tight smile.

"Well, you are an academic of reptiles, are you not?"

"And of amphibians, but I gather you're not interested in that half of things," he played along, taking a glance around at what he conceded must've been the crew.

"Then I would think only one such as yourself could appreciate our operation here," Eve thoroughly failed to explain—or, more likely, refused to—before stepping back into her cabin and adding, "Oh, and, Bruno, see to it that he is made ready." She slammed the doors shut, returning to yelling inane directions to the fruit-bearing lizard on the other side.

Another slam sounded from the side, reverberating through the deck boards, up Dr. Beck's legs, and startling the cat up from its pouch and into his arms. Looking over, he saw the drab monitor and flopped down onto its belly, wearing a most bitterly sullen expression. It glanced up at him grumbling its most guttural hiss yet, before picking itself up and nudging him backward none too gently, nearly causing the professor to stumble over.

"Don't take it out on me, my friend," he said, soothing the cat in his arms, who was also none too pleased by having nearly been taken down with the stumble. "You're the one who brought me here."

Baring its teeth, the monitor produced a deep, resonant growl that could be felt in the bones—every individual bone—more so than heard. It lunged toward the professor, and the man lost his footing, landing hard on his already sore tailbone with all the grace of a toddler. Those dimly purple lips seemed to quirk from a mere threatening display of teeth to a smile as a low, coughing hitch of breaths puffed from the great lizard.

Good lord, was this overgrown monitor *laughing* at him? As if this situation could have gotten anymore appallingly bizarre, the cat, who he was still holding tight, jumped free from the professor's arms and postured up to the colossal reptile, hissing, spitting, and hacking for all his little, damp body was worth. All that served to do was feed the monitor's laughter before it took a swing at the ball of fluff.

Without thought or, quite frankly, sense, Dr. Beck reached out and snatched the cat by the scruff, rolling back out of the way in the nick of time. Laying back, he tried to reconcile with his common sense what had just happened as he dangled the wide-eyed creature above his face. It took no amount of time to realize that such a reconciliation was beyond hope, but it still took him a moment to convince himself to get up anyway before slowly rolling to sit upright. All he could do was give the cat a scolding glare before stuffing it back into the pouch that his waders had become and standing to his feet.

"Well," he said to Bruno, "I believe your master said to lead on."

What was left of its "smile" fell from the monitor's face with a short hiss before it gestured for him to get moving.

It turned out to be "made ready" for whatever this eccentric Eve had planned largely involved getting him cleaned up. For hours, a collection of slimmer, more nimble lizards primped and preened him until he was dressed in dry clothes and his hair was combed and styled, complete with a tropical flower woven into the band securing it back. The clothes were quite dated and heavy for all their layers, but surprisingly sharp and, mercifully, lacking in feathers. After the more physical reworking, they doused him in all manner of floral-smelling powders and oils alongside what seemed to be several, unadulterated spices. Feeling thoroughly like the floor of an apothecary by the end of it, he thanked his lucky stars he wasn't allergic to anything of the sort, because it wasn't as if he'd had a say.

Even the cat wasn't spared the compulsory grooming, which was nothing short of amusing. Many might have thought it cruel to take pleasure in watching the fluffy creature flail as the lizards combed its fur and attempted to tie a necklace of delicate wildflowers around its neck, but there was a certain comfort in knowing he wasn't alone in this weirdness. Not that a cantankerous fleabag was the best of company, but it was something.

Not long after the involuntary prep work was complete, the Sarafina reached whatever destination it was sailing to, and Dr. Beck and his furry companion were ushered back up to the decks. What he saw as he emerged from below was, for once, wonderfully ordinary. He'd half expected this madwoman was dragging them to some secret laboratory where the government was conducting research of the nonexistent sort: a somewhat plausible reasoning he could concoct for the existence of these impossible reptiles currently herding him where they willed. So, needless to say, he breathed a sigh of relief to see a perfectly ordinary limestone beach on the edge of an equally ordinary forested island. There was no telling why they were there, but this place hardly looked capable of industrial evil.

Ashore they were shoved, the professor and the cat, the latter of which was keeping surprisingly close of its own accord. Maybe it considered that any of these large, scaled things could eat it in a single bite and that it was best to keep close with the more familiar, decidedly less murderous creature. Either way, it seemed to carry itself with a certain pride—frosty tail and chocolatey head held high—that the professor couldn't help but admire. Following suit, he straightened his back despite his weary irritation and steeled his expression on what lay ahead. Come what may, he would face it like a man of science and grace.

Short, fossil-filled shelves of blue-gray stone became sandy soil and sandy soil turned to mossy woods, not unlike those at the edge of the marsh. The trees here were younger, at least as far as the forests of the mainland went, possessed of a much spindlier and smoother appearance, aside from plainly being shorter, of course. It wasn't long before the why of that became apparent. A pair of the monitors darted before their prisoners as the trees suddenly thinned, blocking Dr. Beck in his steps just as the foliage vanished altogether. He had a mind to snap at them—he hadn't exactly much to lose—until he looked past their crossed forelegs and saw the precipitous drop there beyond.

It was a quarry: a massive, man-made scar across what was likely the length of the island, cut in cleanly chiseled shelves of a rectangular nature down for quite the distance. The stone of purpose here was clearly the limestone, at one point in time, but, for whatever reason, it was just as clear that time was long past. All that remained, beyond the cut stone itself, to signal the presence of mankind was the dilapidated form of a wooden bridge, long severed by the elements, and the sparse collection of rotten posts that were probably once part of a sort of railing. Other than those pathetic sentinels, nothing separated their company from the sheer drop and Dr. Beck had a horrible feeling downward was their destination.

From the back of the paused pack emerged Eve, still dressed in her feathers but now featuring her own festoons of flowers, which did nothing but intensify the optically offensive nature of the outfit. Without a word, she signaled the hoard forward and onward Dr. Beck and the cat were nudged.

The professor had a wild mind to fight, hardly resigned, even if logic dictated resistance was futile, to plummeting to his death. That pesky preservation instinct was a hard-tamed beast. However, before the notion had more than struck, he saw the thing that put it to bed—the cat was hopping downward upon a flight of limestone stairs. They had no railing and were difficult to make out from the rest of the surrounding stone, but they were broad and seemed sturdy enough. Of course, if he had bothered to spare a thought for why they'd been herding him parallel to the quarry, rather than directly into it, he might've also spared a closer look toward his feet. Funny, the things that slip past the nose.

So down they went, cat taking point, Dr. Beck following close behind, monitors flanking on either side. How far down, he couldn't have said, but it was plenty deep enough for a sense of shade to gather round well before they reached the bottom, where a small stream of pungent-smelling water worked to dig the fissure even deeper.

Gingerly, the cat approached the little river and gave it a sniff before leaping back and clawing its way up into Dr. Beck's arms. At this point, he was hardly startled and, as a matter of fact, nearly found the cat's weight pleasant in his arms. So, that was how they would go. Into the side of the quarry where a yawning, torch-lit cave was carved, the professor carried the cat as the reptilian procession marched him onward.

Whatever had been used to light these torches and fuel their flames was hardly ordinary. They burned with the brilliance that put many electric lights to shame and did so without an offensive odor to their name. Quite the contrary—the cavern smelled intoxicatingly of impossibly indulgent flowers and fruits, sending Dr. Beck's head swimming as he struggled to keep it from flying off his shoulders. It was seeming increasingly likely that this crazed woman was attempting to drug him, leaving him all the more confused when she stepped before him, wearing nothing to shield herself from the overwhelming perfume.

"Well, Brucey," she said, beaming with pride that nearly seemed sad, "just steps from here, your questions shall be answered. May she have mercy upon you."

"I'm sorry, but if I may ask another, simply so I can properly prepare myself," said Dr. Beck, attempting to shake the haze from his head. "Who are we talking about?"

Eve smiled a surprisingly warm smile, looking to him more like an ordinary person than she yet had, one who was awash in wistful regret. "Once, I thought I knew, and I don't doubt you'll assume the same. But, even if it is her name, she doesn't seem to like the sound of it very much. In truth, I wonder if I've ever actually known a thing about her." Turning her back as if to slam the door on any further word, she led on to the deepest part of the cavern.

Here, the chamber stretched to a monstrously massive size, taking on a form that seemed nearly spherical in nature. The torchlight seemed to become amplified, shimmering and shining in dazzling rays that danced through the forest of prisms that grew from every corner of the cave. These were crystals of the purest white and—though this should have been impossible—they broke the yellow light into every color one might see painted across the sky when the sun hit the rain just right. There was something inherent to the sight that made Dr. Beck want to bend the knee and offer reverence, something most unbecoming that painted a curl on his lip. That was a thought for those rock-headed loons in the geology department, though... maybe some small part of him wished some of them could see it—just a spare, tolerable few. No, what was worthy of his awe had yet to reveal itself and, once it did, he thought he'd died and gone to the afterlife he'd insisted had no existence.

Shining, like obsidian dipped in a gossamer oil that shifted with every color—even those it seemed no human eye had beheld—a great, graceful neck rose high above his head, it's ventral scales hardly discernible from the rest save for where the edges caught the light with their fractured mosaic of colors for how perfectly black they were. Atop this neck was a regal, gorgeous head of an arrow shape, set with dazzling, silver eyes framed by wing-like scales that gave its face such a fierceness. He'd hardly noticed the feathers—a near flaw, in his opinion—but there they were, a great mane of plumage draping down from between the eyes and back. These were undoubtedly the feathers Eve wore and, he had to say, she did them no justice compared to the serpentine enchantress before him. It was seemingly coiled inside a nest of these feathers as well, though he could hardly take his eyes from that face.

"My dear, insane woman," said Dr. Beck in utter awe, "all you would've had to do was say the word and I would've come here."

"Hardly," Eve said from somewhere behind him, perfectly in time with a flick of the massive snake's tongue, her voice sounding distinctly different. "Humanity relies far too much on its eyes to hear a truth beyond that which they have already seen."

The professor snapped his head around, earning a discontented growl from the cat at his sudden jerk, to see Eve standing in the center of a bowed circle of monitors. Her eyes were open but empty, her body still as stone.

No, there wasn't a chance. Such a thing wasn't possible. He'd given concession to much of this madness—far too much of it—but there was no basis, no tether to reality, not a *thing* that could possibly allow for what he had to be seeing. And yet, there it was. All he could do was turn back toward the giant serpent with his mouth agape in puzzled horror. What of *any* of this had a tether in reality?

The great serpent tilted its head at him as Eve's voice laughed. The professor petted the cat, thought of it, the serpent, the madwoman, the scurvy crew of monitors, and came to one, singular conviction.

A frown formed as the horror dropped from his face and he gave the serpent a shrug. "Hmph. Fair enough."

"Oh…" the serpent flicked his tongue at him. "I… Are you… are you not afraid?" She used Eve's voice but, somehow—because of course she could—furrowed her own brow as she stooped her neck to look more closely at him.

"Afraid?" scoffed Dr. Beck, an involuntary laugh bubbling through, as he continued to pet the cat. "I suppose I should be."

"Yet you're not…? Yes?"

"Surprisingly, no," he answered, his eyes wandering down to the nest of feathers, bringing yet another impossibility to his attention that made yet another seem entirely too possible. "Tell me, Serpent—unless I should address you otherwise."

"Such an address is permissible…"

"Fantastic. Tell me then, Serpent, do you happen to have wings there?"

"Hmm?" The great snake bent to look down toward her nest, before looking back at him with a profoundly quizzical expression for a snake. "Indeed. Many. Though I must wonder why that would be your first question."

"Mostly because it leads to my next," he answered simply, "Are you a god?"

Raising her nose, she looked askance at him. "So, some would say."

"Great. So that's a no," he noted with a brisk nod.

With a short burst of a hiss, the serpent flinched back on itself, seemingly flabbergasted—hardly becoming of a creature claiming godhood. She flicked her tongue in rapid succession, furrowing her brow at him before shaking her head, her feathers rattling together with a strangely musical quality—like a pit of strings tuning before a show. Afterward, she settled back into her regal air and had her servant speak for her.

"It matters not what your small mind thinks, human, what matters is what I can provide and if you so desire so rare an offer."

"Of course," Dr. Beck scoffed. "Persuade me, then. Woo me into joining your..." He looked back toward the lone, manikin-esque figure of Eve and her band of colorful lizards. "... accomplished cult."

The serpent hissed, but otherwise kept her composure. "Whatever you desire—riches, wisdom, power—I can grant it to you." Darting forward with a shockingly silent ease, she wrapped her neck around where he stood, to stare the professor in the eye with a look that was much too close to hinting at attempted seduction. "Just name it."

"I'm sure," the professor said dubiously, giving the now-trembling cat a slow, contemplative stroke, desperately wishing he could take a step back. The idea of being "desired," as it were, by a snake was far less pleasant than that of being eaten, and he was all too keenly hoping for a third option to appear. "Tempting as it is to sell my soul for grant money," he continued. "I do have to wonder why you would need more than one flesh puppet. I'd think you'd already have more—someone as distinguished and cunning as yourself—if you did."

The serpent loosed what sounded like a weary hiss, the texture of the sound setting the professor's every nerve on end and nearly making the cat leap from his arms. Shooting a withering look over his shoulder, she clarified, "Oh, this is entirely voluntary."

"Voluntary…" he echoed, looking between the serpent and the woman, who now looked to be wearing a slight bit of indignation on her once-blank face. "No wonder you're having such a difficult time. I imagine it's hard to find someone willing to work in these conditions… and in such a uniform."

"No, that was her choice as well," said the serpent, giving a curt flick of her tongue. "Now, if you'll hear me, I'll explain why I wish for you to join me here, why I offer to grant your desires."

"If you must," Dr. Beck sighed.

The entire form of the serpent seemed to expand and subside as she took a deep breath before giving her spiel. "I require a caretaker. One who will see to my needs, body and soul. One who understands and is willing to learn all that—"

"She doesn't know the first thing about reptilian husbandry, does she?" the professor cut her off with a wolfish grin as it finally clicked.

The serpent flinched before dropping her head to the cave floor in a pathetic display of utter defeat.

"No, not in the slightest!" she forced Eve to whine. "The humidity here is abysmal! And have you any idea how cold the winters get? Yet she insists this is where we ought to be—and don't get me started on the feedings! What is it with you humans and sacrificing your own kind? She's not the first one! I could almost overlook it if it weren't for the terrible bone-to-meat-ness of your kind and the infrequency of—"

"*Excuse* me!" roared Eve, sounding suddenly much more like herself, much to the serpent's shock.

Bingo. It seemed Dr. Beck's third option was arriving.

The beautiful beast recoiled back and hissed, her face twisted with rage, as her feathers flared.

"After all this," Eve carried on, marching from the ring of monitors, who were all picking up their heads in confusion. "Everything I've sacrificed and all I've done! I'm wanted in five states!"

"Hardly my problem," the serpent seemed to say through her again before the woman slapped her hands over her mouth, only for the serpent to add, "I tried to tell you the sacrifices were ridiculous. And I've begged for you to educate yourself!"

"*Oh*! You want *education*? How 'bout I teach *you* something?" Eve shrieked, plucking a crystal up off the cave floor and hucking it like a javelin.

The shard struck the serpent on the nose, seeming to glance off as harmlessly as a piece of paper. She gave Dr. Beck the barest of glances, almost as if to ask if he was seeing what she was before immediately going on the attack. Feathers flared, fangs extended, her hiss shook through the cave, shattering several of the small crystals and cracking many of the large. She darted toward the woman, crawling forth on her draping wings as they flared out like massive fans forged from captured rainbows while Dr. Beck stepped aside, covering the cat's head. Somehow, Eve missed being swallowed whole and was fighting back, wielding long shards of crystal-like swords.

"This may as well happen," the professor muttered to himself as he watched what amounted to a battle befitting a Greek myth play out in front of him. "Hell hath no fury like a woman scorned and all." Honestly, part of him wanted to see this play out, knowing that it at least would be an interesting last sight to see, but he remembered the trembling creature in his arms. Adjusting his grip to clutch him as securely as he could, he said to the cat, "I think it's time we made ourselves scarce," and moved to escape.

Along, he shimmied, watching all the while as the serpent would lunge and the woman would dodge, how the woman would slash and the serpent would hiss. Scales, feathers, and shards flew. Every inch of the surrounding stone shook. Monitors were scattered like anoles that had caught the eyes of children. And Dr. Beck was nearing the chamber exit. Once he reached it, he was gone.

Running fast as his desk-softened legs would carry him, he fled, never slowing until he reached the open air. Only for a moment, he staggered to catch his breath beside that foul-smelling stream, the entire quarry shaking around him, before making a beeline for the stairs. Up he sprinted like his life depended on it—and it very probably did—not stopping even once he'd leapt over the top, no matter how his lungs felt they might explode. Forward, forward, forward, back through the woods, over the limestone beach, and into the longboat that brought him from the ship he went.

Getting the boat into the water was another story, as he simply refused to let the cat go until it had nowhere to go but into the vessel. It took him long enough, armlessly pushing and shimmying the boat from the hollow of stone it was perched on, that he was there to witness another impossibility.

Up from the quarry, he watched the great serpent soar on six wings and, just barely, the figure of what must've been Eve on her back. What happened after that was hardly visible, but there was a horrible hiss that shredded the air and the serpent was falling. Her landing rattled the entire island, shaking the boat free into the water and knocking the professor from his feet as fissures formed throughout the fossil-filled limestone of the beach. Without a thought, the professor jumped to his feet, then into the boat, hardly making it to the thing as it was sent jetting off, riding the shock of the impact that produced a gargantuan plume of dust from the center of the island and bent the young trees.

And off he rode, the cat in his arms, watching as the cloud dissipated and the island shrank, the ship, too, shrinking beside it. They were all a spec on the horizon before he let his fluffy companion stretch his legs. The man was given such a sour look for his trouble. Dr. Beck tried to return it but couldn't help but smile. All of this started because of that cat, and, somehow, he'd made it through it all. How many of his nine lives had he spent, the professor couldn't help but wonder. Hopefully, he wouldn't spend the rest of them starving out there on the lake.

Based on the setting sun, they appeared to be sailing south, which was a good enough sign. Dr. Beck had none of his effects, so he had to trust solely on celestial navigation. How barbaric—oh, and how expensive replacing his camera would be. The compass was hardly that expensive, but that camera...

Laying back in the boat, he only hoped he survived long enough to truly be bothered by such an inconvenience.

The cat hopped up onto his belly, curling up in a great, brown heap of fuzz and, for just a moment, the professor thought he might be happy to die just like that.

Die he did not and, in a matter of days, he found himself sitting at his desk, yet again, with Ms. Phoenicia Druce pestering him.

"I'm still not entirely sure you even went and looked," she accused, crossing her arms.

"Oh no, I did," he insisted, not looking up from the paper in his hand. It was hardly an interesting read, but she was far less so. Besides, the faster he got her to leave, the faster he could return to what he actually wanted to read. "It's just I found nothing, and, I must say, Ms.

Druce, you're quite lucky I don't report you for harassing a professor, for I'm not entirely sure you didn't set up an elaborate prank."

"Prank?" she protested with a squeak, taking a stomp forward. "To what, exactly?"

"Who can say what's in your twisted mind?" he said blithely, waving off her protests. "But I can certainly say there's any number of things out there that could've killed me. I, of all people, should know. My word." He finally sat up and set the paper down, giving her the full strength of his best, impish smile. "You could've set something up in that cabin just for that point and purpose and it's only by my lucky stars I missed it."

"As if you'd be worth the effort!" she scoffed, stepping back.

"Oh, but I will be more than happy to write an obituary for your cat to be printed in this month's student paper, complete with my thorough report of all that didn't kill him," Dr. Beck teased rather tastelessly, if he did say so himself, but he really wanted her to leave. "I would be needing his name though, since you didn't care to give it before."

"It's Fiddle, you ass! I can't believe you! How can—No. I can't. Have a nice day." She tacked that last bit on with such a bitter form of cordiality, he was almost impressed, though he would have to take points off for the mighty slam of his door as she stormed out. Having to have it replaced would hardly be a good use of his time.

As her stomping steps faded away, Dr. Beck breathed a sigh and dusted the worthless read from his desk before opening the large door near the foot of the thing.

Out popped the cat, who he finally understood to be named Fiddle—a most fitting name—looking up at him with almost accusatory eyes.

"Oh, if you'd really like to go back with that, by all means, say the word." Dr. Beck gestured toward the door.

The only response Fiddle gave was hopping into the professor's lap and turning on the purring almost immediately.

"That's what I thought," chuckled Dr. Beck, giving the cat a scratch before opening the top drawer and drawing out the tattered old folktale book he'd procured from the library. After all, he had better learn all he could about these feathered serpents before the eggs hatched and the real research began.

Chasing Shadows

Shawn McGee

Shawn McGee is an author based in North Georgia with a passion for speculative fiction, storytelling, and fantasy. His writing often delves into complex moral consequences across mixed genres, weaving imaginative and thought-provoking narratives. His debut Urban Fantasy is available worldwide, and his upcoming Military Sci-Fi/Isekai Fantasy hybrid is set for release in 2026.

When not immersed in writing, Shawn enjoys gaming and working in IT. Chasing Shadows *holds a special place in his heart, exploring themes of personal privacy in a world where digital image sensors were never invented.*

Connect with Shawn and explore his work at https://wartimedruid.com.

What conspiracies lay waiting behind those impenetrable walls?

Caleb settled into position on the cold stone wall. His fingers gripped tiny crevices for support as he scaled the rock. Once the security guard performed his rounds, the cameras wouldn't give an intruder away. Currently, he relied on the darkness. Darkness and staying off the fire escape.

For years, Caleb had gathered piecemeal evidence of corruption linking longtime Senator of Massachusetts, Bruce Fitzpatrick, to an intricate web of murder, bribery, and embezzlement. But concrete proof had always eluded him. Tonight's mission had the highest stakes. Hidden beneath a cloak of secrecy, he knew he had to photograph the people in the meeting. A clear picture on thirty-five-millimeter film. Even the richest of countries couldn't fake pictures without telltale signs on the negative.

The lights of the Kodak building didn't make it to this side of the hotel. There weren't many places where the lights of the largest company in the world didn't penetrate. Kodak's influence dwarfed Boston politics and stayed above the corruption. And now, Caleb would use their light to shine on the corruption.

Every politician had bought and paid for the Boston Globe. While the Herald was not in the hip pocket of the politicians, they wouldn't risk funding an investigation. Caleb's independent newspaper was the safest way to get proof of corruption published. But that required planning, stealth... and luck. Tonight, equipped with only a bag of high-tech gear, Caleb was going for the jugular.

He opened the seventh-floor window and slid feet first into the room, protecting his camera case. The padded carpet deadened the sound. His heavy pack made it through with little effort.

He hid on the floor and listened for the whirring of the camera. Crouched against the wall, he hid much like he did when held his sister the night Old Fitzy murdered their father. His sister, Sarah, had teared up but didn't make a sound. He clung to her until all the men, which included police officers, disappeared. They had to wait all day before reporting the body.

They ruled the two gunshots to the back of his father's head a suicide.

The whirring told him the camera spun away and stopped in its resting place for the guard's monitors. Caleb kneeled on the thin carpet and verified the surroundings. The camera parked, and the guard patrolled. No one else strayed into the alley. He prepared his camera.

Lowlight conditions with a telephoto lens required a lot of hardware along with specialty film. His sweaty hands shook as he pulled out his lens and attachments. Getting caught here wouldn't mean an arrest. The police would beat him and sink his body into the harbor near Quincy.

He took a second and played with the magician's beads in his pocket. It was the best stress relief he had. Out of all the help the family received, one mandated therapist told him he needed a hobby to blend in. Running the newspaper for his family wasn't enough to convince people he was not a threat. He practiced being a magician, even if he never became good. The beads reminded him that others knew what happened and cared.

He checked his pack. The sealed envelope with a magnesium trap stayed sealed. It had a panic location and a code phrase to enter. Code words, secret locations, lowlight film, and a case to protect his camera from view.

Police and politicians tried to enforce regulations for cameras. The First Amendment rights on film pictures had been under attack and crumbled.

Sarah currently snuck into his basement to move the printing press to the cabin. Her husband had a repossession business. They all hoped it was enough cover. Going after the corrupt politicians meant death was the best option.

Risk became irrelevant tonight. This would be the night he'd capture corruption on film. He'd be the hero to stop the next atrocity. It was too late for his father, who died knowing how much Bruce Fitzpatrick took in bribe money.

He set up and stared at the room in the other building. He needed to keep still. The guard would be back at his post now watching the cameras. He'd be at his post for another forty-nine minutes before his next round.

Senator Fitzpatrick would be here tonight. He'd taken a week of leave to mourn his murdered wife, Elizabeth. Caleb had found no dirt of extra-marital affairs or any sign that he wasn't an ideal, loving family man. The week of mourning was over, though, and old Fitzy had to get back to his job of corruption.

With his gear ready, he crawled to the far end over the thin carpet, out of the range of the guard. All signs showed the plan had worked. The surveillance camera couldn't turn far enough to see through this new window, but he kept his ears open for the sound of shutters and advancing film in the security camera. That would mean life in prison. The cops knew they'd get a conviction with camera evidence, and, once convicted, they'd dictate the prison sentence.

Worrying about getting caught would not help, and Caleb focused on the task at hand. With the lens on, the film advanced, and his focus set, he grabbed the most important attachment. Kodak had partnered with the Sarafina company to write tagging data permanently on the film. The attachment gathered GEO tracking data, camera signatures, and biometrics of the owner. This conclusively identified every picture.

He snapped the Sara Model One to his camera. Pictures held up in court, but pictures with the Sarafina tagging were the gold standard of proof. It was also the gold standard of a brief life. A camera with a Sarafina attachment and objects labeled as spy gear were something you did not want the Boston police to capture you with. The authorities considered specialty gear for journalists, like the egg in his bag, to be insurrectionist tools. Still, he kept them and verified they were ready for use.

He gently opened the window and peered across the alley to find his mark.

Through the viewfinder of his specially modified Canon FLS 180F, rigged for infrared surveillance, the scene came into stark clarity.

The unmistakable figure of Old Fitzy emerged from the shadow. A quick lowlight click with no flash captured the senator perfectly.

The senator closed the curtains as the room lit up behind him. Caleb had to get into that room. One photograph would not be enough to bring down the corrupt Senator.

Caleb pulled his hat down to cover his face. With his bag secured and camera protected around his neck, he peered out the window to verify the security. Time was too short for every bit of stealth. He needed some luck because he would have to use the fire escape to get to the other building.

The surveillance camera whirred to life and swung left. He watched the camera and stepped onto the ledge. Gripping his camera tightly, he wound his way down the rusted metal fire escape. Two floors lower and still out of camera range, he slid the board between the two buildings. Then he crouched and crossed the alleyway and pulled the board back with him.

This building stayed illuminated by the yellow and red Kodak lighting. Every movement was a cautious crouch. The move to the first window lingered forever until he got his hands on it.

Locked.

Sound carried through the walls. A violent struggle with muted cries got loud quickly and became silenced.

Caleb's journalistic instinct kicked into high gear. Information was his highest priority now. He prepared the panic beacon secured in his pocket; one flip of the switch and his sister would prepare an extraction.

Handling his gear with the delicacy of a bomb squad expert, he pulled out his knife. His Kabar opened the neighboring window a crack. Inside, a door connected the two rooms, but an enormous snake guarded it. This serpent had two-inch fangs.

Something was going on in the next room that needed to be captured, and Caleb got an idea. He closed the window and crawled to the one where Old Fitzy had closed the curtains. His trusty Kabar got the window open a crack. The fighting in the room grew in intensity and would give him cover. He'd use the egg to distract the snake, then dash in and charge through the door. With quick hands, he'd snap the pictures and exit through the window.

He wiped the sweat from his hands and prepared his camera. With shaky hands, he reached into his bag and grabbed the egg. He turned the knobs on the egg to high pitch and bright flashing lights. After opening the window, he tossed the egg in and leaped into the room. With a powerful burst, he charged past the snake and through the connecting door.

Senator Bruce Fitzpatrick, a woman, and another man stood next to a beaten and tied up man. Another man lay on the floor, barely moving. Two more men with brass knuckles stood over them, bloodied.

Caleb snapped two good pictures and kept snapping as he retreated to the window behind the curtains. He dove onto the cold metal of the fire escape.

In that instant, Caleb's future was sealed. He'd grabbed the proverbial third rail.

A scream shattered his focus. "The friggin' snake bit me!"

The assailant bitten by the massive serpent guarding the room scrambled after him in a rage. Then the man's screaming intensified and the immediate pursuit stopped.

"I don't care! Kill that guy!" yelled Old Fitzy. "He's a journalist!"

Did the senator recognize him? He was one of the last few independent newspapers in the Northeast. Adrenaline pumping, Caleb covered his lens as he ran. He hurled himself from the fifth-floor ledge onto the precarious fire escape of the third floor, inches ahead of grasping fingers. He descended three stories in seconds and hit the alley in a roll, camera case secured.

Sirens screamed in the distance. Caleb ran like the devil was behind him into the Boston night. In this shadowy game of power, integrity and truth were the real enemies. His actions tonight scared Old Fitzy. From this night forward, Caleb would be running for his life.

With each step, Caleb could feel his heart pounding in

his chest. The distant wailing of sirens served as a constant reminder of the danger he was in. He had stumbled upon something big, something that could expose the corruption that ran deep within the city's power structure. But now, his own safety was at stake. He had no phone for geopositioning or tracking; the Sarafina model had GPS location for tagging of the film, but Kodak didn't pay for constant monitoring. Still, Caleb couldn't let his guard down. He had to keep moving, keep running, and stay one step ahead of his pursuers. The darkness of the night provided some cover, but he couldn't rely on that alone. He needed a plan.

He ducked into the parking garage of one building and up through another. A stairwell gave him a reprieve to flip the panic beacon in his pocket. Next step meant learning the code phrase for his sister. He reached into the pack and used his thumbprint to disarm the magnesium trap on the paper letter. The code, which kept the other safe should the enemy capture one of them, randomly combined words. His contact would say: "Milk the fruit with care." He would answer: "The milk of human kindness."

Two minutes later, a van rolled up. His sister drove it with a smile. She pulled near him. It wasn't as close as she usually parked.

She said the phrase: "Juice is the enemy of the state."

She used the wrong code. They had his sister. For all intents and purposes, he became a criminal. He tossed his panic beacon into the window and ran. He was on his own.

"Release those photos and your sister dies!" screamed a man behind him.

The man chased him as the van squealed away. Shots rang out but towards the van. He could only pray for his sister.

Caleb would not stop. His life was over if he got caught. Sarah's life was in jeopardy already. The corrupt officials had killed his father. Sarah would never forgive him if they lived, knowing they could have avenged their father and chose not to. The only thing to pay for all of this was bringing down the corrupt senator. And he only had a precious handful of seconds head start on the new man.

There was one move in front of him.

He'd have to break into the Kodak building, develop the pictures, and register the negatives in Kodak's data store itself. Once registered, he'd get the pictures to the Herald.

He ran to the nearest train. The 'T' could get him a few stops safely, with a little luck. If they didn't know what stop he departed, his plan allowed him to circle round and stay hidden.

That was his plan.

For now, all he could do was run.

That Was the End

Bryan Caron

Bryan Caron does everything. At least it seems that way, with degrees in Creative Writing and Computer Graphic Design, a background in film making, and being self-taught in editing and motion graphics. It's also why he left his job of nine years to build a successful creative agency, Phoenix Moirai.

During all of this, Bryan somehow found a way to write and publish six novels of various genres, including a 750-page tome. This would become the first step to realizing his ten-year goal of starting his own publication company. You may have heard of it. Phoenix Moirai's publication hub, Whimsillusion. No? You might want to read the copyright page, then.

Before you do, please enjoy his contribution to his own experiment, That Was the End, *while he takes a break at the movies.*

I.

When I was twelve, I dreamed of having a dragon.

I had pictures of dragons, statues of dragons, and many, many dragon toys.

But I never had a real dragon to call my own.

I begged and pleaded with my father, "Please, oh, please can you find me a real dragon?"

"No, son," my father said. "A real dragon would eat you alive."

Then one day, wandering nearby my father's cabin, I found a precious little egg.

It was all alone in some brush, sparkling, and glowing, and smelling of raspberry fruit.

I couldn't believe it; I knew exactly what I had and that was the end of my wish.

II.

I brought the egg back to the cabin and ran to my room with haste.

It was a glorious site to behold, and I would cherish it forever and ever.

But I needed to hide it from my father; keep it out of sight until it hatched.

I hid the egg under my bed and kept it warm with blankets piled high.

When I was alone, I would talk to it and sing to it like a friend; a father.

My own father would ask, "What are you doing in your room so much?"

"I am creating a play," I would tell him with a sheepish grin.

My father wasn't sure what to say to that, so that was the end of the inquiry.

III.

It took days and days, weeks and weeks, and still the egg
sat silent.

I wondered for a time if the egg was real or if I had imagined it all.

No, it was real as real can be, but what if the egg was
something else?

A Faberge egg, perhaps, that someone accidentally
dropped while hiking?

For some time, I thought maybe I needed to do more for
the egg—but what?

Anything, so long as I milked the fruit with care.

Then one day, there was a crack... and then another... and
then another.

Soon, pieces of egg were flying everywhere, and that was
the end of the egg.

IV.

Magnificent wings spread out in all their glory; truly a
sight to behold.

It was as big as a cat, or larger than a small dog, if you will.

The name I chose for my new pet, Sarafina, fit her majestic

teal dark green coloring.

I kept Sarafina hidden in my room and fed her as often as
I could.

My father asked, "Why are you eating so much?", to
which I replied, "I'm a growing boy."

He bought it (for the time being), but I knew it wouldn't last.

Sarafina, you see, continued to grow and grow, and soon
would become the size of a car.

What will I do when she no longer fits in my room? I
asked and that was the end of her youth.

V.

Bigger and bigger even still, Sarafina flew from the cabin
each day in search of larger game.

She would always return, though, to the cabin as the sun
faded beyond the mountains.

Taking up the entirety of the floor, wrapped around my
bed she lay.

But the noises at night also grew unsustainable, and my
dad grew much too curious.

One morning, he sat just outside the cabin and saw the
shadow soar into the distance.

He followed it the best he could, all the way to the cave a

few miles away.

Dark and dank, he explored with caution, the scent of
smoke tickling his nose.

Soon, his heart leapt from his chest and that was the end
of my secret.

VI.

He ran back to the cabin just ahead of Sarafina gliding
back into my room.

"Where did it come from, Bruce?" my father asked,
holding my arms tighter than a vice.

"She's my friend," I said, trying to break free of my father's
grip. "She won't harm me."

My father pulled me from the cabin, serious to a fault. "I
asked, where did it come from?"

"From the woods," I said, afraid for my friend. "Near the
cave down the hill."

"Near the cave down the hill?" my father repeated, his
eyes burning with fear.

Then a roar came from the distance, and fire ravaged the
skies above.

They painted the land in flame and ash and that was the
end of the cabin.

VII.

My father frantically searched for a way to run as everything burned around us.

I tried to run for Sarafina, but my father wouldn't let me out of his arms.

But then I saw, with great enthusiasm, the shadow of my friend flying into the smoky night.

She was only a quarter of the size as the beast above her but was still frightfully impressive.

Sarafina joined the other among the forged clouds, united in a familial bond.

But no amount of love or celebration would keep her from completing her mission.

The glorious beast, the size of a jet plane; she was not done with us, not in the least.

She descended upon us with fury and that was the end of my father.

VIII.

I cried. I hurt. I screamed.

Sarafina landed at my feet as her mother flew back into the darkness above.

"What did you do?" I screamed, tears pouring from my
   eyes. "How could you?"

Sarafina peered into my glistening eyes and tilted her head
   ever so slightly.

Could she understand my pain?

I hit her and hit her and hit her in madness, but she did not
   attempt to escape.

High-pitched wails echoed from above, piercing my ears
   to the point of deafness.

I finally stopped, weary and bereft, and Sarafina rose to
   her hind legs, opening her maw.

And that was the end…
of me.

The Safest
Community

Tom Grimes

Tom Grimes is a technology enthusiast residing in Southwest Riverside County, California. He is a very active community member as well as a professor of cybersecurity at National University in San Diego. In his limited spare time, Tom reads a variety of book genres and watches far too many crime-related TV shows.

Tom's passion for crime dramas started at an early age with an exposure to Edgar Allan Poe's The Purloined Letter *and numerous Agatha Christy novels. He has watched almost every police drama since the sixties and continues to seek out new and exciting shows in this genre.*

The Safest Community *is Tom's first published work (even though he has been writing papers and blog articles for years). The team at Phoenix Moirai challenged Tom to submit an entry for this anthology and it seemed like the right time to enter the writing community.*

LI'L BRO

"Milk the fruit with care," I told Mark as he prepared to drain the gelatinous, milk-like juices from the star apples that had just arrived from Amazon, which he had just halved with an almost machete-sized knife.

"I thought we could just squish them like an orange with a citrus reamer, Trevor?" he replied.

"No. Sarafina tried that, and it made a mess of everything," I informed him. "And she found she had wasted a hundred bucks on her first go 'round. Those imported fruits are stupid expensive right now with all the current tariffs."

Mark nodded and decided to call for assistance shouting, "Hey Alexa, how do I milk this fruit with care?"

Alexa, helpful as always, replied with more detailed instructions than Mark could possibly follow in one go. Before Mark could try again, I asked the AI, "Hey Alexa, how do I milk a star apple?"

Alexa returned a much shorter solution this time. Mark tapped the Show device on his kitchen counter and scrolled through the results to follow the much easier-to-follow instruction set. Once satisfied that he understood the process, he dove right into the laborious operation of scooping out the reportedly sweet fruit from each of the star-shaped sections within the apples.

"Why did you feel the sudden desire to try out this particular exotic fruit, Mark?" I queried, knowing my little brother would, most likely, not provide a logical answer due to the odd way his mind worked. You see, you must understand... my younger sibling was what was termed in the 1960s as "mentally retarded," with an IQ of somewhere between 70 and 80. He wasn't stupid; his brain was just not wired in the same fashion as what we might consider "normal." Mark would get an idea or a desire and almost impulsively had to act on it.

"I saw it on a TV show about some rich guy," was all Mark offered.

"Well, I don't know why watching some rich clown

waste his money on a fruit that may or may not be delicious when ripe is any better than eating a papaya, mango, or any other fairly cheap tropical fruit," I countered, knowing he would not argue but just ignore my opinion. "I think you wanted to try it because Sarafina told you it would be cool."

He responded by tossing a slightly annoyed look over his shoulder. He then finished scooping out the last of the pulp and juices the fruit had to offer.

"It looks like you're almost done, so I believe I will head out for now," I said. "I need to go meet up with my client, Bruce, to discuss his latest business venture. Will you be OK for the rest of the day?"

"I'll be fine," he replied. "Quit treating me like a child. I have been on my own for six and a half months now!"

"Sorry. I just worry about you without Mom or Dad to help you," I replied, noting the way he emphasized the "half" in his independence statement.

"I'll be fine," was his dismissive reply.

"OK. I'll see you next weekend," I said and left for work.

THE WORK

Now, work; that is a whole 'nother story. What a trial it has been dealing with Bruce! I swear, if you looked up narcissistic asshole in a dictionary, his image would not only be there, but he would also have a full-page write-up. He thought everyone needed to follow his orders, including an experienced web designer who knew better than to alienate at least half of his potential clients by adding his "divorce story" to the website's About page. Every time — *every* time — my company sent Bruce his next website update, he would return to his fallback position regarding the About page — "Why are you not telling the story of my divorce and how my ex took my company because of the lesbian activist judge she bought?" Many times, we were not even working on anything related to his About page! Sheesh.

But I digress. As I pulled into my office building's driveway, I noticed that someone was once again parked in the spot clearly marked, *Reserved for Intrepid Web Design.* I wondered why people could not respect reserved parking spots, especially the one reserved for my business these past six years! I found another spot and noticed one of my other clients, Darren, was waiting at the door. I gathered my laptop bag and phone and headed into the building. I greeted Darren with a nod and a muffled, "Good Morning," holding the door for him as he walked in behind me.

I walked to my office located down the first hallway on the left and turned off the alarm before inviting Darren in for a non-scheduled appointment.

"Darren, what brings you in for a visit this fine morning?" I queried, assuming something must be very important for him to show up in-person instead of calling.

"Trevor, you know I prefer to discuss major business changes in person," Darren started. "I have always appreciated your web services, but I wanted to talk with you about an offer I received from one of your competitors."

"OK. What offer and which competitor?" I asked cautiously.

"I was approached by Allan Mitchell from Superior Media Services last Friday," Darren said. "He showed me a snapshot of my website's performance in the search rankings, and I must say, I am more than a little disappointed in how your website is performing."

He laid out a folder with several documents containing graph and pie charts along with a web services proposal prominently displaying the Superior logo at the top. I took note of the exorbitant price at the bottom of the page. Allan was quoting more than twice what I charged to originally build Darren's site, and he was wanting more than $2000 a month for digital marketing services.

Naturally my response was, "Darren, you hired me to design, build, host and maintain your website, not for marketing. If you require digital marketing, I can provide a competitive quote."

Darren responded curtly. "That won't be necessary. I

feel that you should have built the website with rankings in mind, and I should not have to pay for that as an additional service. Allan will take care of everything I need."

Our exchange went on like this for a bit longer, but I could tell there was not going to be any way to sway Darren to stay with me. I thanked him for taking the time and courtesy to drop by to let me know in person (though inwardly, I was thinking — he's firing me; what a dick move, considering he was always late paying his monthly hosting bill and now is willing to pay a small fortune, in comparison to my fee, for another company's services!) and to consider coming back to Intrepid if he decided to make a change in the future. God, I felt like such a needy, desperate clown for even thinking that.

So, Darren took his overpriced proposal, left my office and sure enough, he got into the car that was in *my* parking place! Little did he realize it would be the last time he would discuss a website with anyone.

BRUCE, THE NIGHTMARE NARCISSIST

As I settled back into my work routine, the video call app chimed on my phone. It was Bruce. Remember, the narcissist I mentioned a few moments ago?

"Trevor, I have something urgent to discuss with you," Bruce blurted out before I could greet the phone with my default salutation — "Thank you for calling the most intrepid web designers in the world."

"Hello, Bruce," I responded instead. "How can we be of service?"

"I need to be on the first page of the search results, and it needs to be now!"

"Bruce, you are paying us for web hosting and maintenance, not SEO," I countered. "I can provide another quote for search engine optimization and marketing services if you want to be on the first page of the search results for your industry. I must caution you. It will take several months before you begin to see those results because SEO is a long game, not a quick overnight fix."

"Why can't you make it happen sooner? I am the best at what I do."

"Bruce, I don't control the search results. They are based on how millions of search queries occur from users every hour of every day. We cannot predict what people will be looking for at any given moment with perfect accuracy. All I, or any other web guru, can do is optimize your site for what past searches dictate are the reasons you and your competitors are being found on the Internet. We can give the search results a bit of a nudge with local advertising or paid ads, but you have always told me no when I provide a budget estimate for advertising. Would you like to pursue SEO and advertising now?"

Bruce looked like someone had taken a dump on his desk and not had the courtesy to at least spray some air freshener. "Send me the proposal and I will think about it some more," he responded.

"Absolutely, Bruce! I will have it to your email later this afternoon."

"I still don't understand why I am not on the first page of the search results and why people don't know who I am. I have been doing this for forty years! That damn ex of mine and her attorney just screwed me over in the divorce."

"I understand, Bruce," I said, attempting to mollify him. "Let's see what Intrepid can do to help you get back on top so you can laugh at your ex and her attorney."

That seemed to resonate with Bruce. He thanked me and disconnected our call.

Thank God!

This day was off to a hell of a start. Two SEO complaints in a row. Gotta love being criticized for lack of results for a service my clients are not even paying for! I guess I really need to re-examine my onboarding routine and better manage customer expectations going forward... and soon.

RANDOM THOUGHTS

I leaned back in my office chair, taking care not to move too suddenly and tip over. My wife would not appreciate another visit to the hospital after the bowling accident a few years ago that resulted in a torn groin muscle and weeks of recovery time. My mind soon wandered as I took care of numerous, daily requests for website content changes that flowed through my inbox, most of which were simple and mindless; but that's why I make the big bucks as the saying goes.

I kept thinking to myself, Why do I keep losing clients to these vampiric marketing firms and how can I stop it? Naturally, from watching too many revenge thrillers and serial killer documentaries, my knee-jerk answer was, how do I eliminate them and get away with it? I'm sure Patrick Bateman would have a great solution; or I could get Dexter to follow them around until he found something they did that fit "Harry's Code." But, alas, my strong Christian upbringing kicked in to stop my mind from going too far down that rabbit hole. Lucky stiffs, I thought, little realizing that the future held something in store for several of them that was far too close to my original dark thoughts than I could have imagined.

CLOSING TIME

After what seemed like an eternity, my usual office hours came to an end at 5 pm. I had managed to complete all the tasks sent to me from a large sampling of my 150-plus clients, but my mind was still stuck on losing another client to another firm. I knew I needed to get my mind off Darren and his curt dismissal of my services before I spiraled any further, (remember, I was thinking of some pretty final solutions?), so I decided to hit a local watering hole on my way home that offered loud music and karaoke — the perfect distraction from my current funk.

I pulled into The Cave right as the DJ was wheeling in his equipment, so I managed to be the first to peruse the available karaoke songs. Sadly, most of the listed songs were hip-hop or rap (and I use the term "songs" loosely for both categories). I did manage to locate a few songs from my youth under the Classic Rock category, however, and took my turn up on stage. A smattering of polite applause followed, and I almost felt happy when I left the bar several hours later.

MORNING ROUTINE

I woke up the next morning with a slight headache, but not enough to prevent me from attending one of my favorite monthly events — the Chamber of Commerce's networking breakfast. I went about my morning routine: bedside stretching, a bathroom stop for bladder relief, fresh-brewed coffee downstairs while watching the news, and most importantly, walking the dogs with my wife, Cathy.

Our morning walks were a great time to catch up on family doings and other gossip. Cathy enjoyed our morning chats as much as I did. I sometimes wondered if the only reason she stayed with me is to have a sounding board. She was a gorgeous lady; I definitely hit out of my league when I first asked her out. She also did not need me financially as she was a very successful, smart business-person with a small chain of discount stores. Surprisingly, she said, "Yes," and our first date turned into many more, culminating in a marriage of several decades now. I count my blessings every day that I am her husband.

Upon our return to the house, I helped unleash the dogs, showered and dressed for the morning breakfast event. I thought, maybe I will meet a new client to make up for the one I lost yesterday. I grabbed my keys, name badge, and Rotary pin, and kissed Cathy as I paced quickly through the front room and out the door to my car.

FAIR GAME?

The drive to the morning mixer was uneventful and I arrived with plenty of time to spare, parking close to the restaurant where we all would meet. I was warmly greeted by the Chamber staff as I entered and instantly began networking with other business owners I knew well. As more people arrived, I encountered a few new business owners that wanted my take on how well membership in the Chamber was working for my business. Naturally, I answered in a positive, affirmative manner (no one wants to work with a negative personality, right?) and poised questions regarding their business as well. For some reason, I have an almost unnatural ability to tell when someone is truly interested and not just "kicking the tires," and all my new acquaintances appeared to be future customers.

As I headed over to make my breakfast selections at the buffet bar, I felt a tap on my shoulder and a raucous, "Hey brother, how ya' doing?" shout over the din of the room. It was Allan.

"After the stunt you pulled with Darren," I replied curtly, "you ain't my brother."

"What do you mean, Trevor?" Allan retorted with a rather obnoxious grin on his smug face. "I merely pointed out to him that he could do so much better working with Superior instead of what he had been doing for marketing."

"I really don't see how you feel that way when you and I both know you don't move the needle at all for your clients' search results. You just promise the moon, take their money and move on to the next sucker with your marketing pitch. There is plenty of business in this area without you poaching my clients. So, how about you just stay away?"

"Hey, all business in the valley is fair game," he offered lamely as he moved away from me to chat up another potential client.

"Hey, Trevor," a familiar voice said. It was Walter, the city's business development manager. "I overheard what Allan said to you about all being fair game and such. I really wish someone would knock some sense into that guy. He makes it very difficult to sell anybody on what a great place it is to do business in the area. Believe me when I say, I would not shed a tear if he got creamed by a bus a la *Final Destination*."

"Pretty brutal and graphic, Walter," I said. "Maybe karma will catch up to him some day. He has poached several clients in the past year and every one of them regretted working with him."

"Yeah, we can only wish and hope that Death has plans for folks like him," Walter said cheerfully. "And soon."

"He did the same thing to me before I changed from web design to promo," a new voice chimed in from behind us near the stage. As I turned, I was greeted by James, a good friend and ally in the networking arena. James had been in the promotional products field for as long as I had known him, so this was news to me.

"Really?" I said. "I didn't know you used to offer web design before."

"Yeah. I was spread a bit thin trying to offer everything to everyone back then," James said. "That made my website clients pretty easy game for clowns like Allan, Gary, and a handful of other 'SEO Gurus' (James actually used finger quotes for this) that have plagued our industry. I have been so much happier providing a specific service and being less of a target for those jackals. If I was still in your line of work, I would probably have resorted to violence by now. My wife and I are certainly less stressed nowadays. Let me know if I can be of help with keeping the hacks away from your clients. I still have a few ideas on how to get back at guys like that."

"Thank you," was all I could say. "I really appreciate your support."

The rest of the networking breakfast was unremarkable. I touched base with each potential client once more before leaving to let them know I would be calling to discuss their upcoming projects in the next day or two. Then, I headed into work to finish my seemingly constant list of website maintenance requests. Once I was caught up for the day, I decided to break for lunch and headed home for a change of scenery. I arrived feeling positive about my business future, especially with the over-the-top support of my allies, wondering, would they really help me get back at Allan and others, or was that just hyperbole?

Lunch was a simple sampling of leftovers from the last few dinners, and I mulled over how I could recover from the loss of these clients. Also, I needed to come up with a plan to stop losing clients to guys like Allan. Maybe my networking friends would really be the solution. With these thoughts stuck in my head, I decided to head back to the office.

On my way back, I called my little brother to let off some steam. He was an attentive listener as always; although, I was never 100% certain Mark understood most of the social implications that I described to him as it relates to business. He eventually diverted the conversation to how delicious the star apple pulp and juices were and said he would save some for me to try at my next visit. Strangely, he also mentioned that he had picked up a new pet snake named Rita and could hardly wait for me to meet her. Such an odd duck, my brother.

After ending the call, I kept thinking about the conversations I had at the breakfast. Something in the way each of my friends had mentioned death or getting back at Allan just felt weird. Allan was definitely the exception to most rules regarding civility, but I could not, in good conscious, wish mayhem on anyone. Maybe it was nothing, but I felt an incredible sense of foreboding.

UNEXPECTED COMPANY

The rest of my workday was pretty bland — following up on possible new business and fulfilling additional client requested changes to their websites, including a belly dancing site for one of my extremely needy clients. No, it's not what you may be thinking; it's really not as fun or glamorous as you might imagine. This woman was really proud of her looks and did not have a clue that the work she had done on her face over the years was not gaining her any new clients. Yet, she continued to have me upload new images to replace anything older than a year because she wanted to maintain a "fresh, youthful appearance" on her website. Yeah, not so much, but hey, she pays on time.

Sitting back, I looked up and found that it was almost 5 o'clock. Quitting time! Suddenly, there was a knock on the door. It was a pair of gentlemen wearing suits and ties. One looked a lot like Officer Nolan from *The Rookie*, and his partner had a fairly close resemblance to Tubbs of *Miami Vice*. Both looked quite stern.

"Are you Trevor Grimm?" Tubbs queried.

"Yes. Who are you and what is this concerning?" I

replied curtly, moving back into the office and allowing the men sufficient space to enter and close the door behind them. As far as I knew, I had no outstanding tickets, warrants, or other reasons for detectives to come looking for me.

Nolan was all business. "We are here from Murrieta P.D. I am Detective Sergeant Lockwood, and this is my partner, Detective Doakes. We need to ask you some questions about your whereabouts today and how well you know some of your business associates."

"After attending the Chamber of Commerce's networking breakfast this morning, I have been here in my office all day," I volunteered. "What is this concerning?"

"Do you have anyone that can verify your location today?" replied Doakes, ignoring the interrogative portion of my answer.

"I don't know," I responded. "I didn't notice anyone else when I came in and no one has dropped by the office so far."

"So, no one can vouch for you being here all day?" Doakes probed.

"The building has cameras on the main entrance," I replied quickly, but I couldn't resist being a smartass. "Although, I suppose I could have crawled out the window to evade being caught on camera." I immediately regretted that last statement when I saw Doakes raise an eyebrow in interest and look my physique over as if he was evaluating that possibility.

"We'll get back to that in a moment," Doakes said as he shifted his questioning. "How well do you know Walter from the city?"

"I interact with him at chamber events and ribbon cuttings," was my reply. "Why do you ask?"

Doakes didn't answer and continued to his next question.

"Have you ever witnessed Walter lose his temper, be violent or threaten anyone?"

"No, that is behavior I would not expect from Walter," I stated. "He is more of a joker, like a class clown. He's not violent at all."

"Hmm," Doakes pondered. "He has never stated that he would like to see someone get hit by a bus before?"

Aw, now I know where this was going!

"His quips are a bit morbid sometimes," I opined. "But he is just joking. He wouldn't harm a fly."

"Odd sense of humor for that one," Doakes said before continuing. "How about your friend James, the promotional products guy?"

"James?" I responded. "Seriously, where is this going? James is a well-known and respected vendor in our community and is very professional. Why are you asking about him and Walter?"

"Just checking up on all possible leads for our current

case," was all Doakes allowed. "We'll let you know if we have any more questions. And we'll have to check the cameras and your window escape route theory," Doakes calmly stated. "Before we can rule you out as well."

"Rule me out?" I challenged. "Rule me out for what?"

"Murder," was the carefully delivered answer from Detective Sergeant Lockwood. I noticed he watched my reaction intently as I backed up against my desk in shock.

"What... who was murdered?" I asked in bewilderment. After all, this was Murrieta, proudly listed as the second safest city in California. Violence only happened by accident or when hoodlums strayed over the city border from our southern neighbor, Temecula.

"One of your customers," replied Doakes looking down at his notebook. "How well did you know Darren Timmons?"

"Not well, socially," I managed to answer through my shock. "I built and then managed his website for over six years."

"Is it true he fired you yesterday?" questioned Lockwood. They sure seemed to love double-teaming me, especially when I was still reeling from the shock of finding out one of my longest clients was just... gone.

"H-h-how did you find that out?" I stammered.

"That is not relevant, Mr. Grimm," replied Lockwood. "we're more interested in why he fired you."

"He told me he was poached by one of my competitors."

"Well, that would be the reason we are here," Doakes nodded. "We are establishing possible motives anyone may have in this matter."

"But I don't understand how I can be a suspect," I replied. "Clients come and go a lot in my industry. Surely, you don't believe I would consider murdering a client just because they stopped using my services?"

"We can't offer any opinions at this time," Lockwood stated. "But we have seen some pretty weak excuses for committing crimes."

"Well, I know I wouldn't do anything like this," I argued. "Just check the cameras and you will see I was here all morning after the networking breakfast."

"We will know if your alibi holds up when we review the camera footage our forensic team will gather shortly from your building's management company. Do not plan any sudden trips out of the area until we give you the 'all clear'."

I slowly took the business cards offered from each detective and escorted them to the exit.

WHAT NEXT?

Holy crap! I am an actual suspect in a murder investigation. How will I explain this to Cathy when I get home?

This and perhaps a hundred other questions were jockeying for top position on the racetrack of my mind. It's amazing the odd thoughts that go through one's mind when under pressure. Top of the current list were: Do my clients know I am a suspect? Will this hurt my business? What will I tell my little brother, who looks up to me?

I suddenly had an image in my head of the FAQ toggle section on a website with each of these questions laid out, ready to reveal their answers when I clicked on them. The list seemed to go on forever. I quickly shut that image down and finalized any open files on my computer before locking it for the night.

I was halfway to my car before I realized I had forgotten to set the office alarm. I spun on my heels and went back to the office. Once inside, I forced myself to sit down and regain my composure. It would not be advisable to cause an auto fatality because my mind was occupied with thoughts other than the short road trip home.

After perhaps thirty minutes of what seemed like an eternity, I decided I should be okay enough to drive. I set the office alarm, closed and locked the door, and headed directly to my car. Luckily, it was mostly keyless; no fumbling with keys to open the door or start the ignition. I thanked my luck that I had opted for a hybrid with a few amenities during my last car purchase. I encountered no issues on my way home except a few errant calls. The first was identified by my car's call system as coming from James. I pressed the acceptance button and greeted him. "Hi, James. How are you?"

"Holy shit, Trevor!" James began. "Did you hear that Darren was found murdered; his entire mouth was filled with some type of poisonous foam?"

Stunned that Darren's demise was already becoming public knowledge, I suddenly realized I had not thought to ask the cops how Darren died or how he was found or by whom. It was probably good that I hadn't, as I imagined it would have made me look even more suspicious.

"What, Darren's dead? No, I hadn't heard," I lied, trying to convey a sense of surprise. "What happened?"

"His office admin found him when she went to see why he wasn't answering calls transferred to his desk," James relayed.

"Wow, that must have been a stunner for her," I offered. "What did she do when she found him?"

"She was with him for years and had to be taken to the hospital after she fainted and banged her head pretty badly on his desk when she saw his condition."

"Wait. Did you say foam. What kind of foam? Did it look like he vomited, like from drugs or are you sure it was poison?" I probed.

"I don't know for sure, but that is what the M.E. said when she arrived," James provided soberly. "Whatever it was, we won't know for sure until they get the toxicology back, which may be weeks if the substance is not a common poison."

"How did you find out about all of this?" I queried.

"Well, I have my sources downtown," James began. "You kinda build a few of those after being a well-known and respected businessman for more than twenty years."

He began elaborating about his many city and county connections, but I tuned James out as my thoughts wandered once again. I came quickly back to reality when I almost climbed a curb as I made my turn on Whitewood Road. I told James I needed to take another incoming call so I could think without distraction. Naturally, that did not happen. As I hung up with James, another call came in almost immediately. It was Gary, another competitor in my industry. Unlike Allan, Gary was a pretty good guy and did not intentionally poach my clients. He believed as I did, that there was plenty of business to go around. In fact, he had hired me on a few occasions to assist him with clients that had specific build requirements Gary's team were not as well-versed in as I was. I, in turn, had rewarded him with a few clients needing SEO services pertaining to online ads.

"Tom, I assume you have heard by now about Darren." Gary began. "Wasn't he one of your clients?"

"He was until yesterday," I replied lamely.

"Wow, that is a little too close to home," Gary stated. "Let me know if you need any help from my team, should you need some time off or anything." Hmm, was Gary only offering help or did he have an ulterior motive?

"I should be fine, Gary," I replied, perhaps a little too quickly. I hoped I didn't sound too defensive.

"I just want to make sure you are all right," Gary reiterated. "I know a key part of your reputation is forming a strong bond with your clients."

"You jealous?" I chuckled.

"Some of us are," Gary mused.

"Thank you for that, Gary," was all I could reply. He seemed genuinely concerned and wanting to help. Maybe, my paranoia regarding client-poaching should be limited to just Allan? Time would tell.

When I eventually reached home, I discussed at great length the events of the day with Cathy and proceeded to unwind. Needless to say, Cathy was stunned that anyone would consider me a murder suspect. As she put it, "I'm the one with the red hair and bad temper." We both had a chuckle at that.

WASH, RINSE, REPEAT?

After the events of the prior day, I was really looking forward to finishing up some projects as I awoke Friday morning. The sooner I was able to finish everything, the sooner I could suggest that Cathy and I discuss an extended road trip up the coast to Washington to visit some old friends. Of course, life — or the murder gods — had other plans for my schedule.

As I went about my morning routine, I turned on the news as I sipped my coffee. One of the first local stories was one pertaining to another shocking and grisly discovery — Allan Mitchell, my evil competitor, had been involved in a horrific hit and run accident sometime overnight near The Cave Grill and Bar off Los Alamos Road. This made my ears perk up to full attention mode. That was awfully close to where I turned on Whitewood during my daily commute home at night. The estimated time of death was reported by the coroner as somewhere between midnight and 2 am. The newscasters, of course, described the sheet-covered corpse as mangled beyond recognition. He had been struck from behind as he crossed the street from the bank ATM at the plaza on the south side of the street, heading back to where his car was parked near The Cave. Allan had been lifted completely out of his alligator-skin boots and thrown headfirst into a tree on the other side of the street. The anchorperson was postulating with great relish that Allan's head had exploded upon impact with the tree, killing him instantly. The news also stated that no attempt at stopping was present before or after the accident site, due to the lack of skid mark evidence at the scene. How could someone be that cold or oblivious, I wondered?

As I watched the surreal scene on the TV, my phone rang. I answered absent-mindedly, "Intrepid Web Design. Trevor speaking."

"Trevor. Detective Sergeant Lockwood here," the voice on the phone stated firmly. "We'd like for you to come to the station as soon as you are able to discuss the latest tragedy."

"Why can't we just discuss it on the phone now?" was my reply.

"Well, it will take a bit more time than I care to talk on the phone with a suspect," was Lockwood's rebuttal. "So, you can either come down to the station or we can send a squad car out to pick you up. Your choice."

"I'll head over within the hour." I really didn't need a scene for the Karens in my HOA to start rumors about.

"Honey," I called out to Cathy as I gathered my wallet and keys. "It looks like the cops need to talk to me in person at the station. Please call Roberta, your attorney friend, so she can advise us on our best course of action."

Cathy replied in the affirmative as she came into the room with a stunned look on her face. She started to ask a question but decided to wait until she spoke to Roberta and get all the facts instead of what little I could offer.

Unfortunately, my route to the police station took me past the accident scene where I observed flowers, crosses, and photo tributes already showing up for Allan in front of the yellow crime scene tape. It was an interesting touch of irony as Allan was the least religious person I knew in our community. He definitely believed in "doing unto others BEFORE they do unto you." Still, the whole situation was sad — another husband, father, brother, son, etc. cut down too soon.

ANOTHER DISCUSSION

I arrived at the police station near Town Square Park almost thirty minutes after my brief conversation with Detective Sergeant Lockwood. When I arrived, I checked in at the front desk and was told to wait in the lobby until an officer came to escort me back to the detectives. After twenty minutes or so, Detective Doakes appeared almost out of nowhere.

"Trevor," Doakes said flatly. "Follow me." He led me through the door and down several hallways and cubicle lanes until we arrived at what I was pretty certain was an interview room, complete with one-way glass on one wall reflecting our images as we entered, and a table in the center with several chairs on each side. Lockwood was seated in front of the mirrored wall. He rose upon my entrance and motioned for me to take a seat on the other side of the table. Doakes stood directly behind me. Naturally, I followed his suggestion and sat down.

"Mr. Grimm, we have some good news for you," started Lockwood. "We have reviewed the footage from the security cameras at your office building. Your alibi for yesterday is solid. But," he continued, "we have another problem entirely today."

I can hardly wait to hear this one, I thought bleakly.

"We need to know where you were last night and early this morning, say between 11 pm and 3 am. We would also like to take a look at your cell phone if you don't mind."

At that moment, the interview room door opened and all eyes turned to observe Roberta — the "Shark Attorney" — enter the room. Roberta was a local criminal defense attorney that played Bunko with Cathy and friends once a month.

"I don't believe my client will be complying with that last request unless you have a warrant, detectives," Roberta stated flatly. "Have you advised Mr. Grimm of his rights yet?"

When both detectives looked down sheepishly, Roberta continued. "I thought not. I will sit in for the rest of this interview to ensure my client's rights are observed properly." Roberta laid her bag on the table, took out a legal pad and pen, and sat in the chair next to mine.

"Trevor, do not answer any of their questions unless I nod or tell you to do so," Roberta cautioned. "We want to be certain that you don't respond to any inappropriate questions that may lead these detectives to believe you are the perpetrator they are looking to place in custody."

With Roberta protecting my interests, I fielded most of the questions the detectives peppered me with, including where I was during the hours surrounding the hit-and-run's timeline, if I had a good relationship with the victim (hello, client-poacher?), if I knew of anyone that held ill will for Allan (his previous clients, competitors, maybe his family if they were honest, I thought quietly to myself), and what trucks I owned. Apparently, Allan had been hit by the truck at a fairly high rate of speed. Because of how late the accident occurred, there were no witnesses, but the ATM across the street had captured a blurry image of a speeding full-size pick-up truck — but did not capture the plate. Unfortunately, the camera had not captured the actual accident, just the approach of the vehicle. It was almost like the driver knew that hitting Allan closer to the corner helped them avoid the camera. I realized with a start that my little brother banked with that bank, too. I needed to remind Mark not to use the ATMs late at night and get cash back at the grocery stores instead.

The detectives also asked me what I knew about

Walter, James, and several clients common to both Darren and Allan's businesses.

"I don't believe I know anything useful," was all I could offer. I wasn't about to throw any of my friends under the bus for comments said in jest. It was looking to me like the detectives were desperate to find some suspects and get this case solved quickly... maybe too quickly.

Once the interview neared its end, the detectives asked if I knew what a murder-for-hire was. I looked at Roberta. She nodded approval to answer that one.

"Only what I have seen in movies," was my reply.

"And can you tell us what the mechanics of what that would be?" asked Doakes.

"Do not answer that one, Trevor," interjected Roberta. She seemed to feel they were at the beginning of a dangerous fishing expedition with that question.

"Detectives," she continued. "I don't believe any citizen could answer that question without you assuming they were guilty of something. Of course, my client has no idea what the mechanics, as you put it, would be for a murder-for-hire."

With that question stopped in its tracks, the detectives declared the interview completed. As before, they advised me not to leave the area on any sudden trips, especially none out of the state or country. I assured them I would not, and Roberta and I both took our leave.

As we walked out of the station, Roberta advised me to be careful about who I talked to in the coming days, and to say nothing regarding my opinions or what I may have heard about these cases. She really felt the detectives were not done looking at me as a suspect yet. I thanked her for her quick response time, to which she replied with a gleam in her eye, "Tell Cathy I am looking forward to some more of her lemon bar cookies at the next Bunko party."

"I'm sure she will be more than happy to bring a batch," I said as we waved goodbye.

Man, was I ever glad I was not spending the night in jail, pending a bail hearing. Sometimes, it is good to meet and know people through your local Chamber of Commerce. When my membership bill comes in next month, I was definitely renewing.

AGAIN, WHAT NEXT?

Needless to say, my mind was not on my work for the rest of the day, but I still had to pay the bills. I managed to muddle through and stay on top of everything in as professional a manner as possible before I called it a day around 4:30 pm. This time, I remembered to set the office alarm before heading to the parking lot. As I pulled out, I asked my phone to call Roberta's office to see if she had any updates on the investigations. Roberta had no news, so I assumed all was well for now. If the police wanted to pin any of this on me, I am sure they would have had an arrest warrant in the system already that Roberta could see, just in time to really ruin my weekend. I still wasn't able to head up the coast with Cathy like I had hoped.

Next, I called Mark to see how he was doing. He didn't answer, so I left a brief message requesting a call back. I thought it might be a good idea to visit him to reinforce my concern for his safety, especially with the latest happenings around people I knew. I didn't believe there was a connection, but I wanted to exercise caution until the police had someone in custody. I had already had a discussion with my wife during lunch to be more observant and stay home with our two large dogs, Thor and Lady Sif, until I arrived. Yes, I was a bit overprotective. Cathy is a very self-sufficient woman and more than capable of handling herself in almost any situation. In fact, there was this one incident relayed to me by my middle son (and later confirmed by Cathy) — some lady had pushed her cart towards the cart corral at the local big box store near where we lived at the time. The cart missed the corral and struck Cathy's cherished '82 Camaro Berlinetta.

Cathy cried out, "What the hell, lady?", to which the woman stepped right up to her and shouted threats in her face, talking smack.

As I have learned through the years, no one — but no one — gets in her face or violates her personal space, let alone threatens her or becomes verbally abusive. Cathy firmly pushed the woman away from her, telling her to back off, demanding she explain how she was going to take care of the dent in her beloved car. The woman foolishly came right back and tried to slap Cathy's face. Cathy caught her hand mid-flight, twisted the woman's hand down and spun her around. Then, she sent her falling forward with a swift kick to her more than ample ass.

The woman got up and tried to rush Cathy with her arms spread wide and head down as she lunged forward, but Cathy sidestepped her feeble attempt at a wrestling spear, causing the woman to trip over her own feet. Still, the dumbass wanted to continue. She got up, came back at Cathy, calling her a variety of names, and took a wide swing at her. Cathy blocked the awkward punch and jabbed once into the woman's face, breaking her nose with a loud cracking sound. Blood exploded all over the lunatic's face. At that point, security had arrived from the store to put a stop to the fight. The woman was given basic first aid to stop the bleeding and asked if she wanted paramedics called. She declined and both parties left the scene.

When I heard this story, I knew I had married the right woman. I would never have to worry about her taking care of herself... but I may need to bail her out of jail someday.

I was interrupted from my musing by the sound of *Pictures of Home* playing on my phone.

"Hey, Mark," I answered. "How are things going?"

"Oh, I'm fine, you know," Mark replied cheerfully. "I was just trying to locate Rita. You know, that snake I told you I got? I've been looking all over for her 'cause her cage is empty, except for a few eggs I found in there."

"Eggs?" I queried.

"Yeah, I guess that's why she seemed kinda fat when I brought her home," Mark said. "It looks like I will have a few more snakes now, unless I don't find her to take care of them."

"Wow, you definitely got a bargain with that snake," was all I could say.

"Yeah, I suppose so." Mark then exclaimed, "Oh, there she is! How did you get out of your cage and what is that mess on the floor?"

"What's going on, Mark?"

"Give me a second, Trevor," Mark requested. "I have to get her back in her cage and clean up this goop on the floor."

After several minutes, Mark came back fumbling to get the phone steady as he brought it to his face to talk. "Trevor, she was on the side of the fridge and I had to grab her before she got behind it. She also had left a gooey mess on the floor."

"Hmm," I replied. "I really need to come over and check out this snake. I just hope you didn't pick up a venomous one by mistake."

"I know my snakes, Trevor," Mark stated indignantly. "It's a common Sand Boa. Also, that's what the snake store told me, too, and they know what they are talking about."

"OK, OK," I replied obligingly. "I'd still like to see it. Can I drop by tonight?"

"Sure." Mark sounded happy again. "Any time."

Cool, I thought. Something to distract my thoughts for a while. I decided I would see if Cathy would forego dinner, grab some take-out, and head over to Mark's for a visit.

THE SNAKE, EGGS, AND EGGROLLS

Cathy was game for not having to cook and recommended Chinese for our take-out. We grabbed plenty for all three of us, including extra egg rolls because I knew Mark loved those. As we pulled into Mark's apartment complex, I did notice what appeared to be a dark sedan shadowing us for most of our short journey. When we parked and exited the Camry, I was unable to locate anything unusual or out of the ordinary parked nearby.

Huh, maybe my paranoia is kicking in again. I decided

to drop my radar and enjoy the evening. We proceeded to the door and knocked.

"Hi Trevor and Cathy," Mark burst out exuberantly as he answered the door. "C'mon in."

"Hi, Mark," Cathy responded. "How have you been?"

"Well, it's a bit lonely without Mom and Dad," Mark stated. "But at least I have a place to live. A lot of folks aren't that lucky."

Cathy took the food and was marching across the living room into the kitchen area when she froze in her tracks.

"Trevor," she called nervously. "What is that?" Her left hand pointed directly at the snake terrarium sitting on a stand near the living room's corner window.

Shit! I had forgotten about Cathy and reptiles. She haaaaated them.

"I'm sorry, dear," I apologized quickly. "Mark just bought it. It's harmless. It's just a small boa." Although, as I looked closer at the snake, I wondered. The markings and triangular head did not seem quite right for any boa I had ever seen in person (or online). I pulled out my phone and used the Snake ID app to see what the AI would tell us.

After a few moments, the app returned a positive identification — daboia russelii or Russell's Viper. Definitely not a common Sand Boa — and venomous to boot!

"Mark," I asked nervously. "You haven't been handling your new pet without thick snake gloves, have you?"

"Always," Mark replied. "I use the ones that go up over my elbows. Even the non-poisonous one's bites hurt."

I then explained to Mark what he had, and I made sure the terrarium's lid was extra secure, placing extra weighted objects on top out of an abundance of caution. I really couldn't understand how the reptile shop could make such a horrible mistake.

"Well," I warned. "You will need to call the reptile store when they open tomorrow morning and let them know about their screw-up so they can arrange an exchange for you."

"What if I don't want to exchange it," came Mark's reply.

"You actually are OK with having a poisonous snake in your apartment?" Cathy asked incredulously. "I won't be coming here very often, if at all, while that thing is here."

"Mark," I started, "you can't just keep a venomous snake. You will need a special permit, and they usually don't just approve those unless you are keeping it for research or commercial use, like milking it for anti-venom work. Also, you would have to have demonstrable experience working with these types of snakes, and an escape plan should she get loose again. And that's not to mention that your landlord needs to be notified as well."

"OK," Mark replied sadly. "I'll call the store tomorrow. But can I keep her eggs?"

"Absolutely not!" both Cathy and I shouted simultaneously.

"OK," Mark followed up. "I'll ask what I can do with the eggs, too."

With that agreed on, we gathered at Mark's small dining table and doled out the take-out. I noticed that Mark took all the eggrolls. Some things never change. When Mark lived in Oregon, we had dropped in for a quick visit on our way to friends in Washington and offered to take him for some dinner at a local restaurant. When we had almost finished our meal, Mark had asked for some pie. I agreed, and he proceeded to order not just a slice but a WHOLE pie! Talk about taking advantage. My brother really knows how to exceed an offered courtesy.

He did make up for it slightly by offering us a smoothie he had made from the star apples and a few other ingredients he refused to divulge — "My own family secret" is what he told us when Cathy pressed for the recipe. They were quite delicious. Mark informed us that if we liked the smoothies, he was going to provide samples to others in the community for feedback. He really wanted to find just the right blend of the star apples and other secret ingredients to make a product he could sell so as to quit his job as a janitor for the city. I told him to let me know when he was ready for a website to sell them online. I even offered to build and manage it for free.

As we were finishing our meal, I noticed Mark's back window was slightly ajar. He went to check on it as my phone rang. It was James. He said he received a visit from the police, and they had quizzed him about his relationship with Allan. James also informed me that they knew Darren had canceled some orders from him previously and were wondering about any other issues they may have had. It really sounded like Lockwood and Doakes are extending their net wider than just the web guy. Who next? Their IT guy? I told him about part of my interactions with the detectives and let him know that Roberta would probably take his case if they dragged him in for an interview. He thanked me and asked me to send her contact info, which I promptly did.

As I hung up, I noticed Cathy and Mark were both watching me with questioning eyes. I explained what James had told me and suggested we call it an early evening so I could get home, rest, and forget about this week and its drama. Maybe Saturday would start off better.

"I've got your back, Trevor," Mark informed me. I didn't really know what he meant, so I just hugged my little brother and prepared to leave.

We both thanked Mark for letting us visit, reminding him to return the snake and her eggs tomorrow. He thanked us for the eggrolls. We both rolled our eyes at that one and headed to the car.

During the drive home, Cathy let me know she was glad the police were at least looking at other suspects. She felt that was a good sign that we were not going to have our lives turned upside down. I told her I was relieved a little bit, too, but hoped that the killer was none of my friends, like James. I really didn't believe he was capable of anything like murder, but both victims really were exasperating people who rubbed everyone the wrong way.

"Trevor," Cathy interrupted my thoughts. "Do you still have access to your parents' old cabin in the mountains?"

"I believe I have the keys in my desk at home," I responded thoughtfully. "I like the way you think. Let's grab a few things when we get home and head there for a staycation. The detectives didn't say anything about a local mountain trip for the weekend. And I would still be in cell range for a short drive back if they need to ask me to come in for another interview."

"Let's," Cathy replied happily.

THE CABIN

As we made the two-hour drive to the cabin located on Eagle Drive, we argued as usual over the radio station. I preferred rock — especially 70s metal — but Cathy could not stand screeching, high-pitched guitar solos, so we listened to a local country station. This was probably a good thing as I was able to think more clearly while I blocked out the songs emanating from the radio instead of singing with them.

The main thought that kept going through my mind was, "How did that reptile store screw up so badly to sell my brother a venomous snake instead of a small boa?" That and the fact that Mark had found the snake on the floor, out of its terrarium, with what could only have been venom on the floor, judging by Mark's description of the mess he had cleaned up. Another thing, as Columbo would have said, "Why was his apartment's back window open slightly?" Did Mark have a visitor that tried to steal that snake and been surprised by its venomous bite, dropping it on the floor for Mark to discover later when he arrived home? So many questions and no clear answers... yet.

Pulling into the cabin's long driveway, I noticed someone had left the standalone garage's door open. It was one of those old-fashioned ones made from wood with a huge spring on each side to handle the lifting and lowering of the heavy door. I remembered fondly that Mark and I had played handball and dodgeball as young boys using that garage door as a backstop. Once our parents had passed on, we didn't come up here as often, other than to perform basic maintenance on the yard and gutters. We had discussed selling the place from time to time, but it was one of the last remnants of our parents' existence, and Mark refused to let it go.

I walked over to the garage as Cathy took our weekend supplies and belongings into the cabin. I noticed immediately as I entered the deep, foreboding structure, that our dad's old pickup was parked towards the back part of the garage. Odd. I always left it outside or just barely past the door so we would have access to the workbench at the back of the garage and still have room to maneuver for any projects we might be working on with the table saw, lathe, or drill press.

As I went around the front of the pickup to see how close it was to the tool area, I happened to look down and noticed a rather large dent in the grill and bumper. It also looked like someone had hit an animal and left some of its fur and fluids behind. Mark must have been driving after taking his meds again and not been going slow enough to watch for wildlife. It had happened before, so I would have to remind my brother about using a ride share when he was 'up on the mountain' as he called it.

"I guess I'll have to back it out to the driveway and clean it off," I mused.

I looked for the keys in our usual spot — the key cabinet on Dad's old workbench — but they weren't there. Hmm. Next, I checked the usual cliches — on top of a tire (nope) and driver's side visor (not happening). Eventually, I located the keys on the passenger's floorboard like someone had been on a joy ride and just tossed the keys in the truck as an afterthought. As I backed the truck up, the engine made a little bit of a fan belt whining sound before settling into normal running mode. Once settled in the driveway, I pulled the hose over for a quick spray-off. The goop on the bumper came off quickly with the high-pressure hose nozzle.

After cleaning up the mess, I pulled my phone out and called Mark. He answered on the third ring.

"Hi, Trevor," he answered cheerfully. "Whatcha' doing?"

"Mark," I started. "Did you leave the truck up at the cabin?" Of course, the more I thought about it, I wondered how he would have gotten back home if he left the truck up here. Something was not adding up.

"Of course," Mark retorted with a touch of attitude in his voice. "And then I flew back down here on the back of an eagle." Sometimes, his sarcasm was a bit much.

"Just checking," I informed him. "I found the truck inside the garage with the door still open. When was the last time you were up here to use it?"

"That's weird," was Mark's reply. "I haven't been up there for a few weeks. Is everything OK in the cabin?" That reminded me — Cathy was in the cabin alone!

"Shit, Mark. I've got to go," I blurted out abruptly. "I'll call you back."

I raced out of the garage and ran for the cabin as fast as I could. "Cathy," I called out loudly as I flew through the entrance. "Are you OK?" Silence returned for what seemed an eternity.

Then, Cathy rushed out into the hallway from the bedroom area. "What's going on?" Cathy demanded as she tossed a bottle of water at me. I let her know about what I found in the garage and my brief call to Mark.

"I thought the door being open out there was odd," Cathy began. "But I figured Mark might have forgotten to close it. I haven't noticed anything out of place in here so far."

"Well, with the mess on the front of that truck," I noted, "I am starting to think someone is messing with us, maybe trying to frame one of us. That is, if that was hair and human blood on the bumper."

"That's not the least bit funny," Cathy responded with a serious look on her face.

"I'm just kidding," was my lame reply.

"Well, after your visit to the police station," Cathy reminded me, "I would hope you know this is no laughing matter."

"Noted," was all I could offer. "Mark said he hasn't been up here—" That was when my phone rang again. "Hello," I said curtly.

"Trevor!" It was James. "Turn on the local news.

There's a problem at the police station."

Curious, I turned on the old nineteen-inch, box-style television in the living room and tuned it to the local news, fiddling with the antennae to obtain a better signal. The same newscasters that covered Allan's demise were on scene outside Murrieta P.D., announcing that two detectives had been rushed to the hospital after collapsing with foam coming out of their mouths. Samples of the foam had been taken, and forensics had ordered rush testing from the nearest lab to learn the composition of the agent involved. The broadcast also mentioned that the police had also included a sample from an open case (Darren's poison foam) to see if there were any commonalities. "If so," the anchor stated with a gleam in her eye, "we may have a serial killer in Murrieta."

THE SAFEST COMMUNITY?

I was stunned. As I flipped through other channels, I found the story gaining national attention with at least some quick sound bites mentioning the deaths and welcoming our little town to the "ever-growing family of violence." Our quiet bedroom community had made it into the nation's public eye, and not in a good way like when KFI radio had covered our local Rotary Club's Field of Honor display in Town Square Park.

I heard a sigh behind me and realized Cathy had been watching the news as well. "Well, it looks like we aren't going to enjoy our weekend like we planned," Cathy prompted.

"We might be able to salvage some enjoyment," was my hopeful reply. "We won't know anything more about the attack on the police, or if it is related to Darren's death, until the lab results come back. We should try to relax and enjoy some peace and quiet while we can. Let's rent some paddleboats and chase each other around the lake like we used to when we were dating."

Cathy's expression brightened at my suggestion and nodded in the affirmative. "Let me make some lunch to take with us and you grab the spray-on sunblock. You know how quickly we both burn." I nodded and headed to our room to grab the sunblock and some towels. Once we had our supplies for a day on the lake, we drove to the launch dock to rent some boats.

DISCUSSION ON THE LAKE

Naturally, we found we couldn't ignore the events of the last few days. After all, there was a killer in our peaceful community and people near us were dropping like flies. Who knows, we could be the next targets for this lunatic. We might have made one circuit, side-by-side, around the lake before our usual playful banter turned to topics related to the murders and the attacks on the police. Cathy and I discussed how only one of the murders was strictly violent and wondered if the poisonings were unrelated to the hit-and-run that took out my nemesis. It was hard, in my view, to tie the killer that used a vehicle as a weapon to the more subtle killer using poison as death's delivery method. Cathy suggested maybe there were two killers. That seemed like a more logical possibility than one killer switching up their M.O. Of course, we were basing our theories off far too many crime shows and Hollywood movie plot twists. Real life was never like the movies… it was usually more twisted.

During our third lap around the lake, it occurred to me that I used to take care of the website and marketing for the reptile store's owner. That was before he had been poached by — you guessed it — Allan. I wondered about that possible connection. Was Allan still managing the store's account when he met his end? The list of suspects continued to grow. While this may have been great for me, it was not going to make it any better for our local law enforcement to apprehend the real perpetrator — or perpetrators. Our town will probably be in a heightened state of anxiety for a while. Everyone will start seeing their neighbors as potential wrongdoers and flood the police with a ton of calls, wasting their limited resources, while the killer continued their spree unabated.

Cathy pulled me out of my fugue state by mentioning that Mark had given her a pitcher full of the smoothies we enjoyed at his apartment the other night. She pulled the pitcher out of her basket and made a dramatic show of pouring two glasses for us to drink, toasting Mark's potential as an entrepreneur. He would definitely require a lot of guidance on setting the business up, especially the health code requirements, city licensing, banking, shipping, and so forth. As I mentioned before, he tended to be quite impulsive with his ideas, and this would certainly be no exception.

After we finished our drinks, we both felt refreshed and paddled faster to return to the launch point. We tied off the rental boat and headed back to the cabin for what I hoped would be a quiet and relaxing rest of our day. We both agreed we needed to turn off or mute our devices, including the television, and just enjoy the weekend. For once in my life, I actually did just that. No checking in on websites, client emails, or social media posts. The rest of the weekend was a quiet, relaxing blur of time well spent with the love of my life.

BRINGING IT HOME

The weekend was just what we both needed to calm our nerves, but as we awoke on Monday morning, we knew we had to return to reality and all the drama that was going on in the real world. We packed in silence, both of us grinning like teenagers, remembering the way each other felt and moved the night before. It was a blissful euphoria that only long-time married couples could relate to — falling into a routine that negates some of the original romance in the relationship, then suddenly spending quality time together and rediscovering why you were together. Moments like these are amazing for rekindling submerged feelings and strengthening the long-time bond.

As we entered our tract of homes, my phone notified me that I had an incoming call from an unknown caller on the car's screen. I tapped the screen. "Good morning, this is Trevor." I was not quite back in business-phone mode yet with my answering of calls.

"Mr. Grimm," came the voice on the phone. "This is Murrieta P.D. calling. Please hold for Chief Prado." Before I could reply, I was placed on hold with an elevator music version of *Eye of the Tiger.*

Cathy and I were just starting to feel the rhythm of the song and singing to it when we were interrupted by the chief of police. "Trevor," Chief Prado proclaimed in his best public-speaking voice. "We have the lab results back from our detectives' and Darren Timmons' misfortunes. They are both a match for the liquid substance found in each of their systems." He paused for dramatic effect, then continued. "It is our understanding that you used to handle the local reptile shop's website until they moved over to Allan Mitchell's company. How was the transition from your company to Allan's? By that, I mean, was it amicable or contentious?"

"Well, I am never happy to lose a client, especially to someone who exaggerates his capabilities like Allan, but I also firmly believe in leaving the client relationship on a good footing to allow the door to be open should they want to come back." I paused for a breath. "I guess what I mean is, I don't burn bridges."

"That is good to know," replied the chief. "Did you know Allan had just been fired by the reptile store and that they were taking him to small claims for non-performance of his promised deliverables?"

"This is the first I am hearing of that, but not surprised," was my response. Wow, I thought. Karma had finally caught up with Allan finally for poaching clients. "Allan had a reputation of over-promising in our industry."

"Interesting," Chief Prado noted. "Back to the toxicology report. It was a blend of semi-exotic fruit juices, cinnamon, jalapenos and a particularly nasty poison found in only one species of snake, Russell's Viper." He paused again to gauge my reaction.

My voice must have sounded stunned and confused when I asked, "They drank poison?" because the chief responded with, "Not on purpose, I assure you. Darren has been described as full of life and not likely to commit suicide by his family, peers, and co-workers. Neither of my detectives were suicidal, either. The only way they could have ingested the poison that killed them was if they drank or ate something that was tainted with a large dose of the venom. The problem we are having is we are not quite sure how the venom was introduced. And this particular venom can take up to eight hours to cause enough damage to a human to be fatal. This leaves a lot of time to backtrack movements to determine where the victims received the venom. Sometimes, the symptoms can be misdiagnosed and ignored by a victim, so the timeline could be even longer. We need to start with a possible local source for the venom. How well do you know the owners of the reptile store?"

"Only as well as most of my business relations," I replied hesitantly. "I try to be friendly with my clients, but not too personal until we get to know each other better."

"Well, we are going to need whatever contact information you have for all the owners. We need to interview each of them to get to the bottom of these murders," Prado went on. "For some reason their company only lists one of the owners' contact information. It turns out it was to the grandfather who passed a few years ago. No one at the store has any way to reach the remaining owners as they are usually at the store with the manager and other employees and did not provide their numbers. Not even to the manager for emergencies. Odd practice. No one has seen them for several days. We are almost positive that one of them will be our perpetrator. We would like to take them into custody before anyone else dies."

I told the chief I had just arrived home and that I would call back with any information I had in my client files once I was in front of my computer. He said he would be waiting and ended the call.

Cathy and I just sat in stunned silence. I was wondering why he didn't mention any relationship between the poisoning and the hit-and-run that took out Allan. Maybe, the police were thinking one of the reptile store owners lost it, poisoned Darren for a yet unknown matter, ran down Allan for being Allan, and then decided to go after the detectives who were getting too close in their investigation?

The thing is I knew they were absolutely wrong after hearing everything the chief had imparted to me, because *I* knew without a doubt who had done it.

The Bet That
Changed Everything

Duane L. Martin

An avid reader from a very young age, Duane L. Martin frequently dreamed of writing a novel of his own. In 2013 he finally hit upon an idea that turned into the 22 book Unseen Things *series, as well as two other standalone titles—* Cindy's Story *and* The Accidental Hero.

In the early 2000s, he started his own b-movie review website and created a monthly online magazine that focused on independent films.

A great lover of music, Duane began playing bass in 1987, and since then he's picked up some small proficiency in other instruments, including guitar, keyboards, and hand drums. It's a rare thing indeed for him to work on his writing without some sort of music playing in the background.

Born and raised in Northern California, Duane is currently living in Idaho with his wife, Sharon, and their two dogs, Rusty and Kiyoshi.

"Hey, Sarafina. You got time for quickie?" Daryl asked as he pushed his friend through the door of the small salon that she operated out near the edge of town. It was across the street from the auto shop that he and his friend worked at, so they'd run into each other quite often during lunch hours at the cafe a few doors down.

"A quickie?" she asked, cocking an eyebrow at him.

"Bruce here lost a bet, so now it's time for him to pay up."

"Oh? What kind of a bet?" she asked with a grin.

"They bet me I couldn't go one day without bitching about a customer," Bruce explained.

"Huh. How long did you make it?" she asked.

Daryl suddenly snorted and giggled. "Go ahead. Tell her," he said.

"Eighteen minutes. Almost nineteen," Bruce grumbled.

"Wow, that must be some kind of a record," she said with an amused look. "So, what's the penalty for losing the bet?"

"Still gonna be business in the front, but the party in the back is over," Daryl explained. "Need you to just sorta lop it off, right about… here."

"You're really gonna go through with that?" Sarafina asked as she walked over to examine the back of Bruce's mullet.

"Well, I lost the bet, so I guess I have to," Bruce said with a heavy sigh. "Seriously though, this ain't even fair. It's not my fault she drove with her check engine light on until her engine seized up. What kind of an idiot does that? You'd think she'd change the oil at least once a century, but I guess that was too much of a bother."

"Bet that's gonna be expensive," Sarafina said as she led him over to the salon chair and had him take a seat.

"She's just gonna have to get a new car. Replacing the engine is more than the car's worth. The whole car smelled like death anyway. Should just take it out back and set it on fire."

"Death? What do you mean?" She draped a cloth over Bruce and secured it at the back of his neck. She then proceeded to pump the lever below the seat repeatedly with her foot to jack up the chair.

"God, it was horrible. I got in the car to try to start it, just to check out the situation, and the whole interior just reeked of death."

"What would make it smell like that?" she asked, wrinkling her nose a bit at the thought.

"Wasn't just the car either. *She* smelled like it, too," Daryl added. "I can't say I was surprised that he bitched about it when he got out of the car, but she was still standing over at the counter signing the paperwork."

"So, what'd she say?" Sarafina asked.

"Nothing," Daryl said. "She just got all embarrassed and left. He was really goin' off about the smell though, so I'm not surprised."

"I think I pieced it together after she was gone," Bruce said.

"Oh? She been transporting corpses for the mob or something?"

"No, but you're close. She was transporting one for her dog."

"What do you mean?"

"Well, judging by all the dog hair in the car, I'm guessing she was a frequent visitor to the dog park. Probably didn't think nothin' of it when she called her dog back one day and it had a squeaky toy in its mouth.

Thing is, it wasn't a toy, and it sure as hell ain't gonna squeak no more."

"So, what was it?" she asked.

"Dog left a dead squirrel sitting on the floor in the back, and then I guess it kicked it under the passenger seat while it was getting out of the car. God knows how long she's been driving around wondering where the hell that smell's been coming from."

"Oh my god, that's just... ugh!" she said as she suddenly felt her stomach churn with disgust.

"Anyway, long story short, that's how mister party in the back here lost the bet. So... here we are," Daryl added.

"Might as well just cut my whole head off while you're at it," Bruce said as he shot Daryl a dirty look that amused him to no end.

"Awww, come on now. It won't be so bad," she said consolingly. "I'll make it all nice and neat for ya'. Next time you go out, you'll have to beat the ladies off with a stick."

"He's already been through that, only it was the lady's husband he had to beat off with a stick. Actually, it was a pool cue he beat him off with. Left a nice little knot on his forehead, too," Daryl explained as Sarafina retrieved her scissors and comb from the sanitizing container on the counter.

"So, you were messin' around with another man's wife?" she asked, cocking an eyebrow at him.

"I didn't do anything! Well, I didn't do *that* anyway," he said defensively. "See, I was pretty damn drunk at the time, and I guess she was all pissed at her husband, so she came over and sat down next to me at the bar. Then she started actin' like we were hookin' up or somethin'."

"And you didn't do anything to encourage it?" she asked.

"I was half asleep when she came over. Hell, I was so out of it, I didn't even realize she was talking to me. I thought she was talkin' to someone on the other side of her. Anyway, next thing I know, her husband yanks me off the barstool and takes a swing at me."

"So, what'd you do?" she asked as she combed out the bottom of his mullet and began snipping away at it.

"I lost my balance and fell over backward onto another guy who was just walkin' by. He grabbed me to hold me up, and then that chick's husband took another swing at me. Only, I fell down again, and he ended up hittin' the other guy. Things got a little blurry after that, but Daryl said that when he came in, I had a busted pool cue in my hand, the husband was lying on the floor unconscious, and the place was all tore up like there'd been some sort of a massive brawl."

"Oh, you should have seen it," Daryl said with an awe-struck look. "In the aftermath of battle, his mullet backlit by the lights of a neon beer sign, he stood there drunkenly over the body of his fallen enemy with a busted pool cue in one hand, and bruised knuckles on the other. My god, it was absolutely majestic!"

"Wish she'd have left me out of her marital issues," Bruce grumbled.

"Well, look at the bright side. At least she didn't smell like death," Sarafina said with a grin.

"Even if she did, I was too drunk to notice," Bruce said, cringing a bit as he felt the scissors hacking away at his pride and joy.

"There we go," she said a few moments later. She grabbed a hand mirror off the counter and held it up behind him so he could see the results. "Whatcha' think?"

"I don't know," he said dejectedly. "Hey, Daryl. What do you think?"

"I think you look like a dork, but at least you don't look like someone who'd go cruisin' for drunk chicks in a beat up, rusty old El Camino anymore, so I guess that's somethin'," Daryl said flatly.

"Very funny," Bruce said with a comical sneer as he pulled his hand out from under the cover to flip him the bird.

"Hey, what the hell does that mean anyway?" Daryl asked, ignoring him completely as something on the far wall suddenly caught his attention.

"You really don't know what that means?" Bruce asked as he waved his middle finger around a bit.

"No, that." He pointed at a poster on the far wall of a cat hanging upside down out of a tree. The caption at the bottom said:

Milk the fruit with care.

"Oh, that?" Sarafina asked as she looked over at where he was pointing.

"Yeah. What's that mean?"

"Dunno. I found it at a thrift store when I opened the place. I was looking for some decorative stuff to sorta... you know... spruce the place up a little, and I thought the cat was funny, so I bought it."

"What the hell does that even mean though? It makes no sense," Daryl said with a confused look.

"Means whatever you want it to mean, I guess," Sarafina said with a bit of a shrug. She removed the cloth that was covering Bruce and then lowered the chair so he could stand up. As soon as he was on his feet, he reached up to feel the back of his head. The look on his face was absolutely heartbreaking.

"What do I owe ya?"

"Nothin' sweetie. This one's on the house. You've had a rough enough day as it is," she said with a sympathetic smile.

"Well, thanks. How about if I buy ya lunch sometime instead?"

"Sounds good," she said as the boys headed for the door.

"All the guys are gonna laugh at me when we get back over to the shop," Bruce said.

"So… just another Tuesday, then," Daryl said, laughing as he opened the door. Bruce smacked him on the back of the head in response, but he didn't try to dodge away or anything. He knew he deserved it.

"See you guys later," Sarafina called after them.

They both turned to give her a quick wave, and then headed back over to the garage.

Smiling to herself, she grabbed her broom, swept up the remains of the mullet into a dustpan, and then set it on the counter.

"Poor guy," she muttered to herself as she pulled a small, handcrafted doll from a drawer and secured a lock of hair to it with a silky piece of red ribbon tied in a neat little bow. Holding the doll to her chest, she closed her eyes and stood silently for a moment.

When she opened her eyes, she turned and headed to the back room of her salon where she had a little shrine set up. She gently placed the doll next to several others that were interspersed around a few large candles that, judging by the hardened trails of wax streaming down their sides, had all been lit rather frequently. All of the other dolls that had been placed on the altar had locks of hair tied to them as well. Most were tied with the same red ribbon, but there were also a few that were set apart from the others that had been tied with black ribbons.

"There now. Let's see what fate has in store for you," she whispered to herself before heading back out to the front to wait for her next appointment.

*   *   *

Two days later, Bruce headed back over to the salon. After stopping to spruce himself up in the window reflection for a moment, he stepped through the door. He'd obviously taken the time to clean himself up. He was wearing a nice set of his normal street clothes (rather than the overalls Sarafina usually saw him in), and there wasn't even the slightest hint of grease or grime to be found anywhere on him. As it turned out, he was actually in really good shape, cleaning up far better than she'd expected.

"Well, look at you!" she said with a bright smile as she came over to greet him. "You look great! What's the occasion?"

"I don't know. I mean, I just...," he said, obviously embarrassed by her question.

"Sorry. You really do look great, though."

"Thanks. I was just wonderin'... I mean, if you're not busy or anything, if you'd be up for havin' lunch together?"

"Oh, for the haircut?" she asked.

"No. I mean… like… together. You know… like a lunch date," he said in a halting manner. He looked so bashful; she actually felt bad for him. He'd obviously made a great deal of effort to make himself presentable, which was actually quite flattering.

"Well now, I suppose I could fit that into my busy schedule," she said with a reassuring smile. "My next appointment isn't until two o'clock, so just let me grab my bag and we'll get goin'."

As soon as she headed off to the back, Bruce turned and saw Daryl staring at the salon from the garage. As soon as they made eye contact, Daryl gave him a thumbs up gesture with a questioning shrug. Bruce smiled and returned the gesture, which made his friend endlessly happy. After flashing him a huge smile and a double thumbs up, Daryl quickly headed back into the garage to tell the others.

A few moments later, Sarafina returned with her bag and the pair headed off to the café down the street where they usually ate.

"It's a nice day. Wanna sit at one of the outside tables?" he asked when they arrived.

"Sure. Sounds good," she said.

Bruce escorted her to a table with a large shade umbrella sticking up out of the center. "This all right?"

"Fine," she said, smiling.

He pulled her chair out for her in a gentlemanly fashion that she found rather endearing. "I'll just go and let Janey know we're here, so she can come and take our order."

"Just tell her I want the usual. She knows what it is," Sarafina said. "That, and a large lemonade."

"All right. Be right back," he said as he turned and headed inside. When he returned a few moments later, he found Sarafina talking to something she had cupped in her hands.

"Hey, whatcha got?" he asked as he sat down and stared at her questioningly.

"This little guy decided he liked me, so he jumped off the bush and landed in my hair," she said with an amused look. As she held her hands up to show him, a small lizard poked its head up through the hole she'd left between her thumbs.

"Oh! Hey there little fella," he said as he leaned in to take a closer look. "Seems like he's got good taste in women."

"Seems like you two have got something in common then," she said with a smile that faded quickly when it suddenly occurred to her that she might be presuming too much about the nature of their lunch date.

"Whatcha gonna do with him?" he asked.

"I'm gonna put him back on the bush," she said as she held the little creature up and stared into its eyes. "You believe in reincarnation?"

"Dunno. Why do you ask?"

"When I was a kid, my grandma used to say that when we die, those who've led a good life are given a choice between moving on to the hereafter or living again as someone or something else. Like a bug, or a bush, or even a lizard," she said as she turned and gently released the lizard back onto one of the bush's thicker branches. It sat there for a few moments, looking around as if it were trying to figure out where to go, and then it just scurried away.

"That's interesting. I never really thought much about it to be honest," he said with a thoughtful look.

"Yeah well, she was a special lady. Lots of folks got wrapped up in their local Baptist churches and stuff back then, but there was a community of Asian folk who were mostly Buddhists living near where she grew up. They were all descendants of the old railroad workers and what not. My grandma made a lot of friends there while she was growing up, so I guess she just sort of absorbed a lot of their philosophies. Lots of folks didn't want much to do with 'em, but you know how it was back then. They didn't want much to do with anyone who didn't look like them, no matter what race they were. My grandma though, she loved those folks. Got a lot of great recipes from 'em, too, when she was growin' up. I got 'em all in a book back at the house that she left my mom when she died. Then when I moved out on my own, my mom passed it on to me."

"Sounds like she had a really interesting life. Too bad she's gone. I love hearing stories like that from back in the day."

"She married one of 'em, you know. God, what a scandal that was. Her parents practically disowned her, but she didn't care. She really loved my grandfather, so they got themselves a little piece of land, built a cabin on it, and there they raised four wonderful children together."

"What a great story," Bruce said as he stared into her eyes for a moment. "Wish my story was that interesting."

"What *is* your story?" she asked.

"Grandpa ran shine until the feds finally caught up with him. Grandma was left with pretty much nothin', so she took odd jobs here and there to make ends meet while she raised my father. My dad, he started out as a mechanic, which I guess is how I ended up as one. He saved up his money and bought a junkyard on the other side of town. He's a good man. Always did his best to make a good life for us."

"What about your mom? What's she like?" she asked as the waitress brought out their food and set their plates in front of them.

"Thanks," they both said in turn.

"Can I get you guys anything else?" she asked.

"I think we're good. Thanks, Janey," Bruce said with a warm smile.

"All right. If you need anything, just gimme a holler," Janey said as she headed back inside.

"So, about your mom...," Sarafina said as she picked up her utensils and dug into her meal.

"She was a stay-at-home mom. Always really involved in my schooling. She liked to grow food for us in her garden. Really helped out financially, since it kept the grocery bills low. She raised a lot of chickens, too, so we got eggs and meat from those as well. Man, we used to eat a whole lotta eggs. Guess that's why I grew up a lot beefier than most folks. All that protein, ya know? Well, that... and a lot of hard work. That stuff they make cars out of ain't exactly light, ya know?"

"Apparently," she said with a smile, eyeing the broadness of his chest and shoulders.

"So, uhhh... yeah," he said awkwardly.

"What?" she asked.

"I mean... I'm not very good at this. Daryl was just kiddin' about me pickin' up drunk chicks in an old El Camino. Fact is, I've never actually... I mean..."

"Never what?"

"Like, I've never been with anyone before."

"Never?" she asked with a surprised look. "Not even a blind date?"

"Never met anyone I liked enough to ask, ya know? Most girls never even look twice at me in that way anyway, so I guess I always just sorta figured I'd end up alone."

"So what made you ask me out?"

"Dunno. I mean… I *do* know, but…"

"What?"

"Like, after you gave me that haircut the other day, I had all this newfound confidence all of a sudden. Well, no… that's probably overstating it. I guess I just sorta looked at myself in the mirror, and for the first time in a long time, I was actually happy with how I looked. Seems like that mullet's always been a one-way ticket to the friend zone, so I never really thought about asking anyone out before."

"Can I be honest with you?" she asked.

"Oh. Here it comes. I guess I shouldn't have…"

"No, it's not that. It's just… I mean… I like you. I like you a lot, but there's something I need to tell you before this goes any further."

"Oh, god. You're not a dude, are you?" he asked.

It was such a ridiculous question, she couldn't help but laugh. "No, it's nothing like that. It's just… well, my grandma didn't just pick up on Buddhist traditions. Her mother grew up in Louisiana, so she was wrapped up in some kind of voodoo stuff that grandma never really wanted to talk about much. I guess she saw chickens being bled out in rituals when she was a kid and stuff, and it kinda traumatized her."

"Jeez, no kiddin'," Bruce said as he picked up his glass to take a sip of his lemonade.

"Apparently, things were getting really intense with that group she was involved with, so my great grandfather took her and ran off with her before something really bad happened."

"Bad like...?" Bruce asked as he sliced his finger across his throat.

"Yeah, that kinda bad," she said. "Anyway, my grandma taught me one of the old rituals they used to do, and I still do it to this day."

"You ain't killin' chickens are ya?" he asked. "I mean, when I was growin' up, some of my best friends were chickens."

"No, nothing like that," she said with a breathy laugh. "It's sort of like voodoo dolls, only instead of sticking pins in 'em, I tie a lock of hair or some other personal belonging onto them, and then I close my eyes and pray for something to happen to that person. When someone's a good person, I wish for something good. When they're not, I wish for them to get what they deserve."

"Does it work?" he asked curiously.

"I used a lock of your hair to make one the other day, and now here we are," she said with a smile.

"You wished for me to ask you out?"

"No, nothing that specific. I just wished for you to

have confidence in yourself. You seemed so lost after I cut off all that hair, I wanted to boost your confidence a bit, give you a better outlook. The fact that you used that newfound confidence to ask me out was just a nice sort of a side-effect. I didn't even know you thought about me that way. We haven't really spent a lot of time together other than talking here at the cafe and whatnot."

"I've sorta had a crush on you for quite a while now. I just never thought you'd be interested in someone like me."

"I never really thought of you in that way to be perfectly honest," she said.

He stared down at his plate for a moment, looking rather disappointed and saddened by her words.

"Oh. Okay…" he said quietly.

"But then you showed up today, and the amount of effort you put into making yourself look presentable just so you could ask me out… Well, now I'm thinking of you that way. So, go ahead and pick your chin up before you get gravy all over it. I'm having a really nice time."

"Really?" he asked with a hopeful look.

"Yeah, I am. Maybe next time we can go out on a proper evening date. What do you think?"

"I'd like that," he said with a smile as his heart started doing little backflips in his chest.

"Anyway, now that that's settled…"

Just then, multiple sirens blared from down the street.

As they both stood up to watch, a car blew past the cafe at top speed with several police vehicles hot on its tail.

"Holy crap! What's goin' on here?" Bruce asked no one in particular.

A few moments later, the car the police were chasing tried to make a turn, but the driver was going too fast. He cut the turn too hard, causing the car to flip over. It rolled furiously several times before slamming into some parked cars and coming to a stop.

"Yeah, I know that car. I guess I can take his doll off the altar now," Sarafina said as she sat back down.

Bruce stared at her for a moment, then sat himself back down as well. "What do you mean? Who was that?"

"His wife and I were friends back in school. About a week ago she came in looking like someone had beaten the hell out of her. Turns out, that someone was her husband."

"Oh, my god," he gasped. "So, she asked you to…"

"Yeah. She knew about the dolls, so she cut off a lock of his hair while he was sleeping and brought it with her. I strapped it to a doll with a black ribbon, and then made one for her with a red ribbon, wishing for her to find happiness again someday."

"Jesus Christ. So that stuff really…"

"Yeah, it really works. Come to think of it…"

"What?" he asked.

"When I made yours the other day, I got to thinking

about it after, and I made one for myself as well," she said.

"What'd you wish for?"

"I just wished to be happy. Funny thing is, I set my doll right next to yours. So, I guess it all makes sense now," she said with a thoughtful smile.

"So… you're happy?"

"Yeah, I am."

"You know what?"

"What?"

"I am, too," Bruce said with about the most genuine smile Sarafina had ever seen. He scooped up some mashed potatoes and gravy with his spoon. Unfortunately, in his excitement, he ended up spilling some of it down his chin and onto his shirt. Before he even knew what was happening, she grabbed her napkin and leaned over the table a bit to wipe his chin for him. She paused for just a moment when their eyes suddenly met, and in that moment, they knew that the dolls she'd so lovingly crafted for them, had dutifully fulfilled their purpose.